Big George
and the
Seventh Knight

Eric Pringle

illustrated by
colin paine

BLOOMSBURY
CHILDREN'S
BOOKS

For Pat, who is always there — EP
For Paul and Mary – CP

First published in Great Britain in 2002 by Bloomsbury Publishing Plc,
38 Soho Square, London, W1D 3HB

Text copyright © Eric Pringle 2002
Illustrations copyright © Colin Paine 2002
The moral rights of the author and illustrator have been asserted

A CIP record of this book is available from the
British Library

ISBN 0 7475 5539 7

Printed in Great Britain by Clays Ltd, St Ives plc

10 9 8 7 6 5 4 3 2 1

Big George and the Seventh Knight

Also by Eric Pringle

Big George

Contents

Foreword
In Days of Old when Knights were Bold

For two hundred earthly years the Stranger slept inside the hill. From time to time, his rest was disturbed by dreams – glimpses of a vast, barren landscape of mountains and stones, lit by a colossal, cold sun. The place meant nothing to him, but it bothered him. Even in his sleep it bothered him.

Then the dreams would fade and the Stranger would sleep undisturbed for another fifty years, while outside his sanctuary history moved on and the world slowly changed.

It is the Year of Our Lord 1305.

Tilly Miller and Simpkin Sampkins, who built a shelter over the Stranger's massive frame and planted grass and trees and bushes and flowers, so that the giant structure looked just like a hill, are dust.

Whole generations with their kings and queens and wars have come and gone. Even Richard the Lionheart and the Crusades are only memories, and now King Edward I – called Longshanks because he has legs like stilts – sits upon the throne of England.

But in the countryside things haven't changed very much. There are more people around than there were in Tilly's time, but even so there are three times as many sheep. More ground is cultivated, but there are still great forests and wastes for hunters and poachers and wild animals. And everywhere people still believe in magic.

Daily life in these 'Middle Ages' moves rather slowly. The horse is the fastest transport, and most people don't even possess a horse. All they have to carry them about is shanks's pony, so they don't travel far from home.

Life could do with a bit of a jolt, really. And it's going to get it, because on this warm June evening something exciting is happening.

Listen!

Do you hear that noise?

Do you hear the shouting and barking and neighing as men and dogs and horses go charging through the greenwood? Can you feel the drumming of hooves on the ground?

And look! Who is this running before them, racing out of the undergrowth like a terrified rabbit and making straight for the Stranger's sleeping ground?

Look! Listen! Helter-skelter, here he comes . . .

chapter one
Surprise for Two

When Walter broke free of the forest he had no idea where he was going. His only purpose was to evade capture, for capture would mean trial and punishment – terrible punishment.

The boy's hands bled, and below his short tunic his legs had been torn in a fall. But he didn't care about that. He felt no pain. There was no time to feel pain.

Daylight was fading as he scanned the wasteland ahead. He saw heath and bog and beyond that open fields and a distant village. Nowhere to hide. He needed somewhere to hide.

A small hill on the heath caught his eye. It was curiously rounded – more a hump than a real hill – and it was clad in bushes and low trees and covered by an enormous briar rose in full bloom. The sun setting behind the hill made its flowers blaze like a hundred fires.

There seemed something magical about that, and Walter, whose head was crammed with stories of wizards and warlocks and witches, needed some magic right now. He thought, perhaps the hill will offer me sanctuary. If it doesn't, I'm done for.

He heard the hounds baying close behind him – too close – and the sound of galloping hooves and the excited voices of men and of women, too. His lord was there, and his lord's lady, enjoying the pleasures of the hunt. But there was no pleasure for him, because he was the quarry.

Walter's heart cried out to the hill and he ran towards it as fast as his aching legs would carry him.

Its sides were as steep as walls. They were too steep for dogs and horses, which was good, and he had to grab the bushes to pull himself up. Under the shrubs it was already dark, but there was not enough cover for complete safety.

The men might see him, the dogs smell him.

Fear gripped his throat like a fist.

I must go higher, he thought.

He reached for a bush above his head, but to his dismay its roots lifted away from the ground. For a frantic moment he thought he would fall. Then, as he began to slide, his scrabbling feet with their

pointed shoes found a stone embedded in the hillside.

The stone held.

Sobbing with relief Walter looked more closely at the straggly bush and noticed a narrow cleft beneath it. He tugged at the surrounding grass and, wonder of wonders, the grass peeled away to reveal a hole wide enough to take the body of a slim boy like himself.

Walter breathed a prayer of thanksgiving and slipped through the gap like a fox going to earth. He vanished just as the first hound burst out of the greenwood.

Now the hunters appeared. There were a dozen of them, with hawks at wrist, swords at side, longbows slung across their shoulders and peacock–feathered arrows sheathed at their backs. While the dogs spilled about their horses' legs, they looked out across the darkening wasteland. All they saw was a mound, black against a bloodshot sky. And all they heard was a blackbird whistling goodbye to the day.

Walter plummeted down the hole like a stone.

Mother save me, he thought, I'm falling into hell.

But he hadn't dropped very far when he was stopped short by something strange. It was neither hard nor soft but something in between, and under his winded body he felt it rising, and falling – slowly, slowly – like waves waxing and waning on a beach.

He thought it might be some kind of quaking bog. He had better move carefully.

It was black as pitch inside the hill, except that away to his right there glowed an eerie greenish light. Swallowing his fear, Walter crept towards it.

The ground beneath his knees felt curiously like fabric, and then – oh help – as he reached out a hand towards the glow his fingers touched something like wire, like bristles, like a beard!

Walter recoiled. He was sure now that he had fallen into the lair of one of the monsters the minstrels sang about in his lord's hall after dinner. But there was no snarl here, no convulsing leap, no terrible snap of slobbering jaws to tear him limb from limb.

Instead, warm gusts of air alternately sucked and pushed him like a wind that couldn't make up its mind which way to blow. And then there was the merest hint of what might have been a snort.

Was the monster sleeping?

Curious, Walter inched forward again – and with a start saw that the greenish light was coming from a face.

But what an extraordinary face! It was

surrounded by hair shaded blue and green and it sent out a light like a lantern.

On top of which, it was enormous – bigger than any face he could ever have imagined. But the strangest thing of all, the thing which made Walter hold his breath with fear, was that although in many respects it looked like a man's face, it wasn't human and never had been.

Walter realised now that he was kneeling on the creature's chest, just below its long – its very long – neck. And to his surprise he noticed a piece of paper pinned to its tunic.

He peered closely in the green glow and saw that it was a note, in scratchy, uneven writing.

It said, simply, 'If found. This is George. He is a grolyhoomp.' Signed, 'Tilly Miller.'

Walter gulped and made the sign of a cross on his chest. What on earth was a grolyhoomp? Was it fierce or friendly? Was this one half alive or half dead? Asleep or unconscious?

He reached for the quiver behind his back and plucked a small feather from one of the arrows. Then, warily, he crawled up the giraffe-like neck, climbed through the wiry beard, skirted the enormous mouth and, taking care not to touch the creature's skin, leaned forward and held the feather under its nose.

He held his own breath and waited for a sign. When it came, the sign was entirely unexpected. The grolyhoomp snored, and in a chain reaction the feather vanished up its nose, produced a sneeze like a thunderclap and Walter, blasted by the explosion, sailed through the air and landed spread-eagled on a foot the size of a very large horse.

Slowly, the feather drifted down and landed on his stunned face.

And the grolyhoomp sat up.

George, who had been immersed in a very deep sleep, blinked and looked about him.

He could see nothing.

George did not understand darkness. For a moment he thought he must be dead or blind, but then he remembered a battle and pain and a small man called Simpkin and an even smaller girl whose name was Tilly.

The thought of Tilly cheered him.

He blinked again to clear the sleep from his eyes and saw two other eyes staring at him from where his toes should be.

It would be hard to tell whose eyes were the most surprised.

George leaned forward and in the reflected light from his face saw yet another very small person.

This one had black wavy hair and wore a short, embroidered, wide-sleeved tunic above scarlet stockings and black, pointed shoes. He looked rather fancy, though knocked about a bit.

For his part, Walter drew his sword. Although he had little faith in its ability to do more than irritate this strange giant, or pick the bared teeth that were bearing down on him, Walter was determined to fight.

Then, with a shock, he realised that the mouth was actually smiling at him. And speaking.

'Gg-ee-oo-r-r-g-g-g-e,' it said.

Walter bowed courteously. 'Walter of Swyre, at your service, sir.'

'Grolyhoomp.'

George was saying hello, but Walter thought

they were exchanging information. He decided to be honest.

'You're a grolyhoomp,' he sighed, 'and I'm an outlaw. Until yesterday I was page to a great knight, but now I have a price on my head.' His lip trembled.

George frowned. 'Ooothmadderwiggley!' he said.

Which meant, roughly, 'But what the blazes are we doing in here? Where *are* we?'

chapter Two
an outlaw called walter

Something – maybe that toothy smile – made Walter decide to confide in George. So, making himself as comfortable as possible on George's knee, he told the grolyhoomp his story.

'My father, sir, is Robert of Swyre, cousin to my lord Sir Neville de Magott. Until recently he was also his steward and I thought his friend.

'For myself, three years ago on my eighth birthday I was sent to live in Sir Neville's household, to be his page and faithful servant. At first I was content enough – although his rages were frightening and I soon found that he could not be trusted to keep his word.

'I learned how to serve and dress my master and carve at table. I studied manners, and how to read and write, and I was learning the duties and accomplishments of knighthood when . . .'

Walter's voice gave way and he broke off his story to compose himself.

George, who had understood not a word, felt the boy's sadness. He also liked his polite manner, so he leaned forward and said encouragingly, 'Hhrobboonglotl,' meaning, 'Tell me more.'

Walter pulled himself together.

'We were all happy,' he continued. 'Sir Neville had confidence in my father and, I thought, in me, too. But then something happened. My lord Sir Neville's bailiff, one Jeremiah Wormscrode – a treacherous weasel who would tear out anybody's throat if it suited him – was envious of my father's position. So he worked against him by stealth, whispering lies accusing my father of treachery, and turned Sir Neville against him.

'My father was tried in the Shire Court, and because the justices were in the Wormscrode's pay he was proclaimed guilty. Luckily, though, before sentence was passed he escaped with the help of friends and went into hiding. Now he's an outlaw. He could be anywhere. Oh, sir, I fear for his safety, for he's a mild man, and gentle!'

It was anger that stopped Walter's story now. He lifted his head and George saw such a fury blazing in his blue eyes that he was startled.

'My father is not guilty of those crimes!' Walter cried. 'He's an honest, true man! But see how fate has turned against us. The name Robert of Swyre is so disgraced that even to speak it is forbidden. His goods are forfeit. My mother is left alone with no one to protect her – she has nothing and is forced to beg for food and shelter. Meanwhile, Jeremiah Wormscrode is promoted to steward and smiles out of his own backside.

'And I . . .' Walter swallowed. 'I too am in great

danger. "Like father, like son," the parson preached, and Sir Neville believed him, too. He sent men to arrest me but I had word beforehand and fled with the few things I carry. Now I'm being hunted to death, although first Sir Neville will try to use me as a pawn to catch my father.'

The boy looked at the grolyhoomp with the light of destiny shining in his eyes. 'But his men won't catch me,' he cried, 'and they won't catch him! I shall save him – his son will clear his name!'

Even as he spoke, Walter's brain was working overtime, and already an idea was forming in his head. Meeting this grolyhoomp was the most tremendous luck – if he could enlist its help on his quest, why, anything might be possible.

But he was tired and, as they looked at each other in the pool of light from George's face, he felt himself slipping into sleep. He must have dozed for some time before he was woken by cramp gripping his leg, yet when he opened his eyes he found the grolyhoomp still looking at him, unblinking, and he had the strangest feeling that somehow, during his sleep, a kind of understanding had arisen between them.

'Will you help me, sir, in my quest?' he ventured. 'I must warn you there will be great danger.'

'Gug,' George answered.

Puzzled, Walter followed George's gaze, which seemed to be fixed on something behind him. As he turned, the bag around his neck moved and something protruding from the top glinted and caught his eye.

It was his pipe.

'Do you like music, sir?' he asked. 'Is that it? You wish to hear the pipe? I have a tabor drum as well.'

'Gug.'

Somewhere in the back of George's mind the landscape of his dream was gathering again. It hovered hazily – stony mountains, a great, cold sun and, nearer, a dried-up oasis.

Nearer still – just in front of his eyes, so close he felt he could reach out and touch it – the mouth of an instrument gave sweet sounds, and above it the fingers of the player moved constantly. But George couldn't hear the sounds and he couldn't tell whose the fingers were. He was flooded with such longing that tears started in his eyes.

'I asked if you like music, sir?' Walter insisted gently. 'If you come with me I will play for you. I plan to earn my living by performing with the pipe and tabor.'

George focused on him again.

'P-p-l-l-a-a-a-y-y,' he mimicked.

23

Walter reached behind for the pipe, then hesitated.

What if the sound carried outside? His hunters would have given up the chase by now, but it would be foolish to take a chance on anyone else hearing.

Besides, he might persuade the grolyhoomp to leave his shelter by *promising* music. And, once outside, he might be persuaded to go further.

'My journey will be a crusade for justice and truth and my father's freedom,' Walter said bravely. 'I should be glad of your company if you would give it, and we would see the world together.'

Walter watched the grolyhoomp's eyes narrow as he tried to understand. He held the pipe halfway to his mouth and waited.

'P-p-l-l-a-a-a-y-y.'

Even though he had enjoyed less than a quarter of the rest required in his own world, George was no longer sleepy. He felt curious about this boy, and edgy too, for Walter's urgency had communicated itself to him. 'P-p-l-l-a-a-a-y-y,' he said again.

Walter nodded. 'Outside, sir. I'll play outside.' He slid down George's leg and jumped off his boot. 'But first we have to find a way out of here. I wonder, could you bend this way, please?'

He beckoned. George leaned forward. As he moved, his face lit the shelter like a swinging lamp, and in that instant Walter spotted a row of wooden hinges on the wall near George's feet.

He pressed his shoulder to the wall and heaved. The earth was cold against his sleeve. He pushed again, straining. 'Help me!' he gasped.

'H-e-e-l-l-p-p.' George raised a knobbly finger and laid it against the wall and the wall moved.

'Gently. Do it gently. We don't want to attract attention.'

George pressed again and slowly the wall opened. Stones clattered down. Stems of grass appeared.

Outside it was night, but there were stars and, in the eastern sky, the first glow of dawn. As they looked out a thrush burst into song nearby.

Walter raised his pipe and played, quietly imitating the bird. Backing through the door he felt the fresh air touch his neck like a soft breath. Fronds brushed his elbow. He prayed that George would follow.

The piping seemed to George to come from inside his own head, where the oasis still lingered. He moved towards it and found himself outside with the bird and the stars.

'Zwolloqmiddy,' he whispered, wishing himself and Walter luck because he suddenly felt they both might need it.

Then, after closing the door so that to passers-by the hill looked only a hill again, Big George followed a young outlaw called Walter into the dawn of a summer day in medieval England.

chapter Three
Into the Greenwood

Already in this first light, men and women were leaving the distant village and setting out to work on their strips of the two great open fields surrounding it.

The fields were a patchwork of colours and crops. On the meadow acres the long, waving flowers and grasses showed it would soon be time for haymaking.

But George had no thought for farming. His experience of humans yesterday – to him two hundred earthly years were only yesterday – had made it painfully clear that these people were not necessarily going to be friendly towards him. They might be small but they could be dangerous, so he knew he had better be careful.

He noticed that Walter was also looking

anxiously at the peasants, and keeping out of sight.

But on this open ground it was impossible for George to stay hidden for long, and when the sun rose up above the horizon the workers saw an enormous, shambling figure, silhouetted against it haloed in golden light.

''Tis an angel!' cried one.

'It's the devil!' yelled another.

'It's big – it's bigger than big – and it's coming to get us!' they all howled together. They dropped their tools and fled back to their homes.

'You're not exactly good news, are you?' said Walter, seeing George properly for the first time. He examined the wiry, blue-green hair and beard, the giraffe neck and the unbelievable bulk of this grolyhoomp. 'I thought you'd be an ally in a scrape, but you'll probably get me into the scrape in the first place just by being there. Still, I asked you to come, so I'll have to make the best of it, won't I?'

Walter peered across a mile of wasteland to the dark line of a forest. It seemed to be empty.

'We'd better get you into those trees as quickly as possible,' he said. 'But mind where you put your feet, George. Try not to leave a trail that a blind man could follow.' To show what he meant he tiptoed forward, and George, who thought this was an interesting new way of walking, followed suit.

'That's it,' said Walter encouragingly. 'Tiptoe.'

'Dd-i-i-bb-doo-o.'

In this way they crossed the wasteland, two figures, forty and four feet high, hunched and hobbling in the morning sun. All the time George was looking around for Tilly, the miller's yellow-haired daughter. But she was nowhere to be seen, and neither was her father's mill. In fact, the entire countryside seemed different.

To be sure, its prominent features were still there

– that far-off line of hills, and the shining river looping around the village – but the details were different. This wasteland, those fields, the houses and the people's clothing were all subtly changed.

Seeing this, George knew somehow that Tilly had gone too. The discovery made him sad, for he would have loved to see her again.

But he was also intrigued by the changes and eager to experience this new world, because after the barren landscape of his dream, it seemed more than ever like a magic land. It teemed with colour and life. George was astonished to see the great abundance of flowers growing, the insects crawling below them, the animals scurrying through them, and the birds flying over them in the bright air. The richness of it all was bewildering.

'Coney,' Walter said, as a terrified rabbit skittered away between George's feet.

'C-c-ooohh-n-eee.'

And 'Sparrow,' Walter laughed, when a brown bundle of feathers hitched a lift for half a furlong on George's head. 'That's a bird.'

'B-r-r-i-i-ddd.'

Once they were inside the forest, Walter was a lot happier. He asked George to walk with his knees bent so his head wouldn't show above the trees, and although George found it hard to bend and tiptoe at the same time, he did his best, because he wanted to please his new friend.

Once George had discovered how to move without making a noise, he found he could hear the sounds the forest made and see its life without frightening it away.

He loved the music made by singing birds and rustling leaves, and the sight of some animals feeding quietly in a glade stopped him in his tracks.

'Those are the King's deer,' Walter whispered, 'and this is the King's forest. If we touch them, we're for it – although later we may have to kill one, to eat.'

Walter was determined to walk all day, to put as much distance between himself and Sir Neville's men as possible. By noon, George found he couldn't stand up if he tried. His knees were locked.

They passed an area where the forest had been cleared to make a cultivated field, an orchard and a garden. Smoke billowed through the open door of a small thatched hovel in the middle of them.

Keeping out of sight, George peeped inside the cottage and saw a woman tending a pot over a fire that was burning on the earth floor. She coughed in the smoke. Outside, a man milked a cow under an apple tree and in the garden a girl was spinning wool. George examined her through the trees, but she wasn't Tilly.

The smell of food made them both hungry.

Walter wondered if grolyhoomps could cook. Somehow he doubted it. He couldn't either, for although skinning and cutting up an animal was a skill pages were supposed to learn, he'd always avoided it because it made him feel sick. Likewise on hunting expeditions with Sir Neville he had always made sure he missed his quarry – although since he was skilled with bow and arrow he was sure he could hit his target if he wanted to.

Walter had to admit that there were many useful skills outside his experience, which he'd never needed until now.

He didn't know how to light a fire with nothing but sticks, for instance, and he wasn't very good at finding his way in a forest.

In fact, he was fairly sure they were already lost.

So it seemed certain that if ever they managed to get some meat they would have to eat it raw. But he did not mention this to George.

At five o'clock in the afternoon George rolled over, felling saplings and groaning and rubbing his legs.

Walter, who had been scouting ahead, ran back in alarm, but when he saw George he burst out laughing.

'You only have cramp, George,' he snorted, 'but you've frightened every animal for miles. Now we couldn't catch one if we tried.'

'Cccc-rrr-aaammmppp. Eeeeyii-yyyooo!' George moaned.

At sunset they camped in a clearing a short distance away from the track they'd been following.

George leaned his back against an ash tree that was smaller than himself and watched the red ball of the sun dip behind the trees. Dark birds winged across it like omens.

Walter, meanwhile, was trying to make a fire by rubbing sticks together on a bed of dry leaves, and getting nowhere. When he saw the grolyhoomp grinning at him, he flushed and offered the sticks to George.

'Here, you try,' he said.

Imitating Walter, George rubbed the sticks between his hands and pulped them into dust, burning his fingers in the process. 'Owww!' he said.

Walter shook his head. 'You're no better than me, George. So what are we going to do?'

Just then, a delicious smell of wood smoke and roasting meat came wafting through the trees.

George's stomach lurched.

Immediately, Walter was moving, beckoning

George to follow. He tiptoed until Walter signalled him to stop, and together they peered into another clearing where two savage-looking men were roasting venison on a spit over a fire.

'Poachers,' Walter hissed – too loudly, for at once the men were on their feet, the taller holding out a knife and the other drawing his sword. They glared towards the undergrowth that was shielding George and Walter.

'Come yowt thur,' spoke the knifeman, softly but clearly, while the swordsman flicked his eyes all round the clearing. 'Come you out and show thyzelf.'

Motioning to George to stay where he was, Walter walked boldly forward. He faced the men, erect and proud.

'Why, 'tiz a boy, just!' the swordsman laughed. 'Only a boy. Kill him.'

His companion grinned evilly, pointed his knife at Walter, and slowly pressed it against his throat.

chapter four
The Bargain

Walter winced, but stood his ground.

'George,' he called, very carefully to avoid impaling himself on the blade, 'it's time to show yourself.'

George thought so too. So he stood up.

And up.

And further up.

He stood straight for the first time in two hundred years, sighed with relief, then stepped forward into the clearing and planted a boot as big as a shed in front of the knifeman.

Gurgling, 'Zave my zoul vrom zider!' the man was instantly and copiously sick.

George brought his other foot forward and held it over the head of the swordsman, who thought the sky was falling down on him.

He fell to pieces. 'Dunna!' he cried. 'Dunna do uz in!' He screeched like a baby, let go his sword, fell to his knees, wet himself, struggled back up again, and ran.

'Noo noo, dunna leave uz!' screamed his sickly companion, and dropping his weapon at Walter's feet he too left the clearing so fast he made more smoke than Walter and George ever had with their two sticks.

Much later, when they had both eaten their fill, and it was night and the embers of the fire were glowing red, Walter looked up at George's shining face and said, 'Sir, I think we should talk.'

'Tt-o-o-rr-kk,' said George, smiling.

'That's right,' Walter said seriously, 'although I could be speaking French or Latin for all you would know. Yet, I think you understand me even so. That's a mystery. You are a mystery. But there's something we must sort out. It's a matter of honour.'

For a moment George looked thoughtful, then he suddenly leaned down low to Walter and with glinting eyes said softly, 'Sordout. Onner.'

'That is correct,' Walter nodded. 'Honour. You see, when a man of honour receives a favour, he must return it. You're helping me, so I must help you. I have nothing worth giving you except knowledge, but what I know I'll happily share with you. I can teach you about people, George, and the world.'

Walter looked at the size of his pupil and marvelled that he had the cheek to make such a suggestion.

George looked at the size of his teacher, and grinned. 'Ffnishhnoddle,' he said. 'Go ahead.'

'Does that mean we have a bargain?' asked Walter.

'Bb-rraa-gen.'

'Not quite. Listen carefully. Bar-gain. Got it?'

'Bb-arrr-gin. Godditt.'

'Good. Now listen.' Walter pointed above their heads. 'That's a tree, see?'

George stared at his mouth, watching the word take shape. 'Tsadd-rrr-eeeezee,' he mimicked.

'It's an oak.'

'Ooh-kkk.'

'Oak tree.'

'Ohkdree.' George's arm speared the branches and a wood pigeon clattered away squawking. 'Bb-rrr-i-dd,' he added.

'That's right! A bird in an oak tree!'

'Sryt. Abbrriddinnannohkdree.'

'Well done,' said Walter, feeling suddenly sleepy as the day's events began to catch up with him. 'That's really brill . . .' He lost the word in a yawn. 'I'll teach you more in the mornnn . . .' His head drooped.

George closed his eyes too, and listened to the night sounds – the rustlings above his head, the patterings in the undergrowth and the screeches,

40

barks and whimpers all around.

Clouds covered the moon and the darkness was intense. He still wasn't used to the dark, and it worried him.

For comfort, George reached into the pocket of his tunic and closed his fingers over a small, hard object – the spoon Tilly had held up to his face so that he could see himself. She had given it to him to keep, even though it had been her greatest treasure.

He took it out, held it close to his glowing face

and fingered the cool, smooth surface. It was tiny and fragile, as Tilly herself had been, and holding the spoon George felt he was holding his friend in his hand.

Holding her memory.

Now other faces crowded the darkness.

All the people he had met in this strange world pressed in on him. Behind them, huge shapes hovered and gigantic shadows walked, drawn by the piping fingers of his dream.

George found them all baffling.

But he knew he must look forward, and above all he must learn. The boy would teach him.

Taking a deep breath, George put the spoon back in his pocket. The faces vanished and he felt better, as if a film had been removed from his eyes.

Now he could give this new world some proper attention. He smiled. It had been a surprising earthly day. No doubt tomorrow would be equally astounding.

He was right.

chapter Five
The Girl in the Pillory

George must have closed his eyes again because the next thing he knew the boy was poking him with a stick.

'I'm hungry again,' Walter said urgently, 'and you must be famished. We could maybe find some berries to eat, but I hate berries, and anyway, I can't see berries satisfying a grolyhoomp. So we must hunt and catch ourselves some real food. But we mustn't be seen. Because if we're caught—'

He drew his finger across his throat.

That was a gesture George understood perfectly.

'Come with me,' Walter whispered, 'but come quietly.'

They tiptoed as if they were burglars, with the top of George's head rising above the trees now and again like a blue-green hairy mushroom.

It was early. Mist floated about the undergrowth, hiding all the birds, deer, wild boar, hares and squirrels Walter sought.

Optimistically, he fitted an arrow to his bow. He was looking for a quarry – any quarry. He had no idea what he would do with it when he caught it. The thought of skinning a bloody carcass nauseated him – but he had decided not to worry about that until the time came.

If it ever came, which seemed unlikely, since behind him the grolyhoomp's boots were cracking sticks like fireworks.

Suddenly, Walter sensed something. He held up his hand and George froze, crouching, on his toes.

A shape moved noiselessly through the trees.

Gesturing to George to stay still, Walter crept after it. Within seconds he had been swallowed by the mist and George was alone in the forest.

He didn't move. He waited.

And waited.

While he waited insects crawled inside his beard and bit his eyes. Cramp gripped his legs. The mist wrapped itself around him like a wet blanket. Still he waited.

Then George heard a cry.

In the mist it was hard to tell where the cry came from – it could have been anywhere. But George was sure of two things: it was a girl's voice, like Tilly's, and she was in trouble.

Walter heard it too.

He had disguised himself with branches in an attempt to look like a harmless bush, and now he was stalking the deer along the narrowest of tracks. It was a noble hart with high antlers, and Walter was excited.

The animal paused between two oak trees, lifted its head and sniffed the air.

With his heart hammering in his chest, Walter raised his bow, pulled back the drawstring, closed his left eye and aimed.

Three things happened.

The first was that, as Walter took aim, his attention was caught by a paper pinned to a tree in front of him. On it was a drawing of himself.

His blood ran cold.

Below the likeness bold letters announced:

**WANTED
— DEAD OR ALIVE —
WALTER
SON OF THE OUTLAW
ROBERT OF SWYRE
REWARD**

Walter gulped. Everybody would hunt him now.

The second thing to happen was the girl's cry. It came from not far ahead and it set the hart bolting, making a kill impossible.

The third thing was as surprising as the others. As Walter turned to go back to George, he fell into a hole.

At first he thought it was a mantrap and he cried out in fear, but it turned out to be just a hole.

It was a very deep hole, though, so deep he couldn't get out.

The girl was making so much noise now that her enemies heard neither Walter's shout nor George blundering through the trees looking for him.

She was tied to a log in the middle of a grassy sward, where three tracks met in the forest.

On a platform facing her stood the jury of twelve men who had decided her fate. Seated on their right were the two justices who had just passed sentence on her, and on their left the verderer, a weasel of a man dressed entirely in green, stood up to proclaim it.

The girl did not care to hear him proclaim it, so she was yelling her head off.

'Stop her caterwauling,' ordered one of the justices, a fat man with folded cheeks and a twitching left eye.

46

The verderer, law keeper of the King's forest, marched up to the girl and raised his hand.

'Dunna yous touch me!' she cried. 'I en't goin' to let yous hit me, so dunna try!'

Laughing, the verderer clapped his hand over her mouth.

She bit it.

Deep among the trees George found Walter, reached down, curled a finger into a hook and fished him out like a tickled trout.

As he did so they heard the shouting change from a girl's temper to a man's agony. Intrigued, they crept forward to see what was going on.

This is what they saw.

They saw the cross-tracks in the clearing and three areas of grass between them.

One held a low wooden frame with two holes in it close to the ground. 'Those are stocks,' Walter whispered. 'They hold prisoners by the legs.'

In the second grassy area there stood a higher, T-shaped frame with three holes in it – a large hole in the middle and smaller ones at each side. 'That's the pillory,' Walter explained. 'I wouldn't be shut in that for anything.'

'Pp-ill-ooo-rr-eee,' George whispered. 'Sshoottt.'

In the third and largest area they saw fourteen men on a platform, a girl tied to a log and a man clothed in green sucking his hand and dancing.

All the men looked shocked and furious, but none of them was remotely as angry as the girl.

She was livid.

'I told 'im, didn' I?' she was shouting. 'I said I en't gonna let nobody come near, now that's ri', isn' it? An' he did, he did!'

She lunged again at the verderer. The ropes held her back, but even so he jumped out of the way as if she were a sword coming to slice him.

She was a ragamuffin, filthy-faced, tousle-headed, shoeless, wearing a dirty, torn blue dress. Around her neck, an ancient rabbit's foot, worn bare with

48

rubbing, hung on a frayed string. She looked about ten years old.

The twitchy-eyed justice scowled at her. 'Verderer, stop licking yourself and proclaim the sentence,' he snapped.

'I will, yer honner, right away.'

Tucking his injured hand under his arm, the verderer gazed up and down the cross-tracks and around the trees beyond them, then shouted in a voice that scattered birds, 'Oyez! Oyez! Whereas the girl Joanne of . . .'

He looked questioningly at the girl. 'Of where?' he demanded.

'Nowhere,' she hissed. 'I told yous.'

'Have it your own way,' the justice sighed. 'Carry on.'

The verderer pumped himself up again.

'Oyez! Oyez! Whereas Joanne of Nowhere has by this Forest Court been found guilty of the felony of coney-catching in the King's forest, and furthermore of stealing a valuable blue shift from my own washing line – how dare she be so impudent as to thieve from the King's verderer? – and furthermore of abusing the King's officers, she is hereby sentenced to stand for three days and three nights in the pillory in this place, with neither food nor water, there to be seen and scorned by all who pass her. May she repent of her sins or else rot. Oyez. Oyez.'

For a moment, the girl's mouth trembled, but she bit her lip to control herself. And this time, when the two biggest jurymen came to untie her, she offered no resistance. She didn't help them by walking, though, so they had to drag her to the pillory with her feet trailing in the grass.

George and Walter watched as the wooden frame was opened to allow the girl's neck and wrists into the holes, then screwed down tight again.

Now she was helpless, a prisoner with her head and hands forced forward, prey to the gaze of jury, justices – and, unknown to her, a boy and a grolyhoomp.

The fat justice approached her, his left eye jumping.

'Have you anything to say for yourself, Joanne of Nowhere?' he asked.

Joanne of Nowhere spat.

The justice frowned. 'Let pelting commence.'

One by one, the jurymen walked past her at a few yards' distance. In turn, they drew from the folds of their clothing rotten eggs and stale vegetables and mouldy cheeses and threw them at her with great force.

Last of all, came the verderer. He walked right up

to her and pressed a raw egg into her hair. Then he hung the carcasses of two dead rabbits, their feet tied together, around her neck.

Not once did the girl cry out. Her head and hands streamed filth, and the skin of her face was raw, but she didn't cry out. She wouldn't give them the satisfaction.

'*Now*, have you anything to say?' asked the justice.

Joanne of Nowhere glared at him. 'Yiss,' she said grimly. 'I hate yous. I hate yous all. All ri'?'

The justice walked away, shaking his head. His

colleague, who had been silent as death until now, stood up and said, 'This court is now ended. Disperse.'

One by one, the men left the clearing and wended their ways along the forest tracks, going back to their ordinary lives.

The girl was left in the pillory, quite alone, and now at last a tear rolled down her cheek.

Walter looked at George, who would have moved much earlier if the boy had not stayed him with his arm, and shook his head to stay him again.

Then he walked out of the trees into the clearing.

The girl watched Walter suspiciously. She followed him with her eyes as he turned this way and that, tormenting her but coming ever closer. Then swiftly he bent to pick up a lump of turnip, threw it at her and missed.

She snarled at him like an angry cat.

Walter threw another, and missed again.

This time the girl laughed, mocking him.

George had seen enough. If this was a custom of these people, he didn't like it. He rose to his full height and stepped forward.

Joanne of Nowhere nearly fainted.

From her bent position what she saw was a tree with legs walking towards her. She craned her neck

52

to see the branches but the pillory prevented her from seeing past George's waist.

'What's *that*?' she gasped.

'A grolyhoomp,' Walter said.

'What's a grolyhoomp when it's at home?'

'That is,' said Walter. 'Although I don't know whether he's home or not. He seems a little lost.'

'Could he get me out of this? I en't happy with it.'

'No,' said Walter. 'You must take your punishment. Besides, we have other things to do.'

He gazed along all three tracks, chose the least worn and set off down it. 'Come on, George,' he shouted, 'leave the girl there. She's nobody from nowhere.'

George watched Walter vanish into the trees, then splayed out his legs, reached down his long neck and looked at the girl upside-down between his feet.

He liked what he saw, even though she was such a mess. He liked the glint of courage and downright stubbornness in her eyes, and he liked the way she refused to show fear.

He smiled at her.

What Joanne saw she could hardly believe. The grolyhoomp's nose looked as big as the pillory, and each tooth in his enormous grin seemed the size of a door.

'Grolyhoomp,' George said, his humming voice vibrating right through to her toes. 'Hello.'

'Same to you, mister.'

George reached out a hand and lifted the pillory out of the ground with the girl hanging from it. Then he set off with long strides after Walter.

Joanne of Nowhere did not cry out.

She couldn't. She was too busy choking.

chapter Six
Joanne of Nowhere

Walter was waiting for George a little way along the track. When he saw the girl his face fell. 'What did you bring her for, George? Now *you've* committed a crime, so there'll be people after you, too. *And* she'll be jumping with fleas, *and* she'll be dead soon by the look of her.'

The girl's face was purple.

'Glug,' she said in a very queer voice.

George hurriedly set down the pillory and with great gentleness broke it open and set her free. Joanne of Nowhere staggered about, coughing and spluttering. She tried to say thank you, but all that came out was 'aks'.

Walter was furious. Although he had been impressed by her courage in the pillory, he couldn't stand the sight of her now. He was training to be a knight, a nobleman, and she was an offence to his sight.

He pushed her away roughly.

'You're free,' he told her, 'so clear off. Go home.' Then to George he said, 'Come on, let's go and find my father,' and marched away along the track.

George followed on tiptoe.

Two hours later, when they paused to drink at a stream, Walter noticed a movement back the way they had come.

It happened again – a flick of foliage such as a small animal makes when stepping carefully.

He fitted an arrow to his bowstring and crept towards the place, his mouth watering at the prospect of coney or squirrel for lunch.

But what he saw when he parted the bracken was Joanne of Nowhere sitting on the track, picking at the sores on her feet.

Walter shook the bracken violently. 'Go away!' he yelled. The girl squealed and jumped and fled away down the track like the startled rabbit he had hoped she would be.

An hour later she was following them again, keeping her distance but not trying to hide any more, her dress a blue blur in the greenwood. Big George kept stopping to look back at her but, every time, she stopped, too.

Frustrated by such erratic progress, Walter approached her again.

This time the girl stood her ground and scowled at him.

'What do you want?' he demanded.

She pointed at George.

Walter frowned. 'You can't have him. He's not for sale. Who are you, anyway? You'd better answer me properly or I'll stick an arrow in you.'

The girl frowned and bit her lip, but seemed to make up her mind to cooperate.

'Joanne,' she said. 'Jo, really.'

'How old are you?'

'Dunno.'

'Where are you from?'

'Nowhere.'

'Don't say nowhere. Everybody is from somewhere.'

'Well I en't,' she cried, her eyes blazing again. 'Leastways, not for a long time I en't. My da was a serf to the Maggot but he died of a fever, and then my ma died of it too, and the Maggot took our house and everything. I was given to another fam'ly, but they beat me so I run away. I bin in the woods ever since, anywhere and nowhere. You tell me to go home, but this is my home.'

All the time she was speaking, she was feverishly fingering the rabbit's foot at her throat.

Walter thought hard. The girl was an outlaw, fleeing from Sir Neville de Magott. That made two of them – three counting George, because you

couldn't imagine a grolyhoomp belonging anywhere either.

'So, what are you after?' he snapped. 'What do
you *really* want?'

Joanne of Nowhere gripped the rabbit's foot
tightly. A light entered her eyes. 'I want to be free,'
she said fiercely. 'And I'm gunna be free, all ri'? I'm
my own person. Nobody owns me. You try to stop
me, I'll tell *him*.' She looked at George and smiled
to herself, as if already he was her friend.

In the Year of Our Lord 1305 most country people
were serfs, or villeins as they were often called.
That meant a lord owned them, lock, stock and

barrel. Everything they had was his – they possessed nothing themselves, not even the clothes they stood up in.

It was in the lord's power to make his serfs free men or women if he chose, but that hardly ever happened.

However, there was another way a serf could gain freedom. This was a custom which allowed runaways to stay free if they could escape to a town and remain inside its walls for a year and a day without being challenged or caught.

Such a feat was difficult at the best of times, and next to impossible for a girl with no means. But Jo told Walter that was what she intended to do.

'So why haven't you gone to a town already?' he wanted to know.

''Cos I been hungry, all ri'?' Jo answered him belligerently. 'I'm always hungry. I gets hungry every day. So I have to stay where I knows I can catch food. Besides . . .' she dropped her eyes in embarrassment, '. . . I en't sure where a town is. And if I en't sure where it is, how can I find it?'

Walter laughed at her ignorance. 'Is that why you're following us? Are you hoping we're heading for a town?'

'Maybe. Are yous?'

'No, we're not.'

'But you might be sometime, ri'?'

'It's possible.'

'Well then, I shall go too. But I'm following him, not yous. I'm going with that grolyhoomp. So don't yous try and stop me.'

Walter could hardly believe a beggar girl would dare to speak to him like this. 'Or else what?' he challenged her.

Nowhere Jo jutted her chin, bared her teeth and turned her fingers into claws. She had very long and very dirty nails.

'I'll fight yous,' she said. 'I can fight all ri'. You want to see?'

Walter decided he did not.

'Suit yourself,' he said, and returned to George.

As they progressed, Jo gradually moved nearer, until finally she was walking alongside George, keeping as close as she dared to his enormous plunging feet and peeking up at his face to see if he showed any objection.

George had no objection. He looked down at her and smiled and said, 'Grolyhoomp.'

'Same to you, mister.'

'His name is George,' said Walter coldly.

Jo grinned. 'Mister George.'

'Dibdoo.' George jabbed a finger. 'Dibdoo.'

'Dibdoo?' Jo viewed with alarm the wagging digit swaying above her head like a gigantic pendulum.

'What's he say?' she squeaked.

'We're supposed to be walking on tiptoe so we won't be heard.'

'Oh. Ri'. Dibdoo. All ri'.'

Giggling, Jo sprang silently forward on the balls of her feet, left right, left right, and then they were all doing it, springing dibdoo side by side through the forest, and it seemed such an extraordinary thing to do that they laughed, and George began to sing because he was happy.

His singing was a thrumming that made the trees tremble.

It was a crooning that shook the ground.

It travelled so far and so fast that for miles and miles all the animals cocked their heads at the same time and listened, and villeins working in the fields and woods dropped their tools and scratched their heads and marvelled.

They thought it was an earthquake. But it wasn't.

It was a Georgequake.

After a while Jo said, 'En't yous hungry?'

'We're starving,' replied Walter.

'So why don't yous catch some food?'

Walter looked away.

'If yous had a coney,' Jo asked sharply, 'could yous light a fire to cook it?'

Walter said nothing.

'Yous might be a gent,' she said, nudging him, 'and he might be a grolyhoomp, but you're both useless. Wait here. Dunna leave me.'

She dibdoo'd away and was soon lost among the trees and bracken.

When they had finished eating charred coney, and Jo had doused the fire and covered the ashes with

dust, she looked Walter in the eye and said, 'It's lucky for yous two I decided to come along, en't it? 'Cos I can find my way in the forest. I can sow and reap. I can cook. I can catch birds, coneys, squirrels, badgers. I en't afraid of anything. I en't even afraid of eatin' snails, long as I bakes 'em first. And I can fish with my bare hands, and light fires the same way. I can steal and not get caught – well, mostly. I bet you can do none o' those things, ri'? I dunno about the grolyhoomp, but how would you ask him? So it's lucky for yous I turned up. *En't* it?'

She glared at them. Walter smiled lamely.

Seeing the look of stubborn determination lighting her eyes, George felt a sudden jolt of surprise. He'd seen that look before, in another person's eyes, and loved it.

He reached out to touch Jo's hair. 'Till-ll-y,' he murmured.

Now it was Jo's turn to be surprised, and not just because the touch of that great hand was gentle as a swan's feather.

'You sayin' Tilly?' she asked him.

George nodded. 'Till-ll-y.'

'Well, let me tell you something, all ri'? One of my ancestors was called Tilly. Tilly Miller. She was my great-great-great-great-great-grand-mother. More or less.'

'Who wants to know that?' Walter sneered.

Jo ignored him. 'I know about her, see, because she's famous in our fam'ly. My da told me a story once about how she found a champion who saved her from a fate worse than death. This is her lucky rabbit's foot. Da gave it to me for luck just before he died.'

Suddenly, she rubbed the rabbit's foot furiously with her thumb and forefinger. She stared at George – at Walter – at George again. Her eyes were full of a wild surmise.

'Don't be stupid,' said Walter incredulously. 'If there's any truth in the story, which is unlikely, it

must have happened – what, two hundred years ago? You can't be suggesting . . .' He looked at George and laughed.

Jo shrugged. 'I know it's silly and I en't suggesting anythin'. I'm just saying, all ri'? But it makes you think.'

She kissed her lucky charm, and moved her lips in a little prayer, and crossed her fingers.

As George watched her, and saw Walter stabbing his sword into the earth, lost in thoughts of his father, he felt a surge of affection for them both. He knew they were troubled – he *felt* it – although he had no idea what their troubles might be. He wanted to help them, but he didn't know how. He decided that the best thing to do for the time being was to stay with them and see what turned up.

What turned up was the toughest man in the world.

chapter Seven
The Toughest Man in the world

The man was an ox.

He was big as an ox, built like an ox and he looked like an ox. He could have pulled a plough with each hand. The muscles on his arms bulged like cannonballs. His sun-browned face was battered as a boxer's after a thousand fights – his nose was flattened so much the tip touched his lip, and his ears were like puffy cabbages on the sides of his shaved head.

He looked a hard and heavy man, yet he tripped silently out of the trees in his short yellow smock and pointed shoes like a ballet dancer on dibdoo, and he surprised them all.

One minute they were resting and he wasn't

there, and the next he was in the glade with them, dappled by leafy sunlight and flailing a cudgel round his head as if he would knock their off heads.

'C'mon then, c'mon then, c'mon then, c'mon then,' he sniffed. 'C'mon an' get it. Who's first?'

Walter drew his sword. He stood firm, feet apart, ready to defend and strike. 'Try me, sir,' he said quietly.

Jo hissed and raised her claws. Her mouth tightened. Her eyes blazed. 'Yous c'mon *here*,' she spat. 'See what yous get.'

George, who was so big the Ox hadn't noticed him, lay still and waited to see what would happen.

Still flailing his cudgel, the Ox stuck out his chin, flipped his bushy red eyebrows and jumped up and down on the spot. Twice. 'C'mon, then' he grunted. 'Don't mess wid me now. Nobody messes wid Peter Bullfinch. I can wrestle bulls. I can box bears. I'm the toughest man in the world – ask anybody at the fairs. So, which of you wants this across his ear first?'

Walter pointed his sword at the Ox's throat. 'I am Walter of Swyre, a knight's son,' he said proudly. 'When I become a knight I shall bow to no man. I shall not bow to you now. I can wrestle and cudgel and ride and fight. I shall fight you.'

'So shall I, you fat Bullyfinch,' Jo purred in a voice full of menace.

They began to circle round him.

The Ox was delighted. He jumped in the air and spun on his points. He grinned. Then he lunged forward and stabbed his stave at Walter, who backed away quickly.

While the Ox was distracted by Walter, Jo darted

forward, jumped on to his back and raked her nails across his neck.

She was down and out of reach before he knew she'd been there.

Then the pain hit him.

The Ox roared with surprise and anger. Blood oozed from the scratches.

'C'mon then, c'mon, try that again,' he sniffed. 'Don't mess wid me.'

George was filled with admiration for this boy and girl. The Ox was so much bigger and tougher than them, yet they were bold and unafraid.

He was ready to go to their aid when Walter suddenly lowered his sword.

Jo gasped.

The Ox gaped. 'You messin' wid me, boy?'

'No, sir,' said Walter politely. 'I would just like to know what you want from us. Because we have nothing.'

Peter Bullfinch blinked. He had never been called 'sir' before. Nobody had ever spoken to him so politely. It confused him. All kinds of thoughts and emotions struggled on his face as he looked at Walter's sword and Jo's claws and felt the blood trickle down his neck.

'I wants that thur,' he growled, pointing, 'for my roof tree.'

Walter side-stepped quickly over to Jo. 'This dimwit thinks George's leg is a fallen tree,' he whispered. 'He wants to build his house with him! Let's see where we can take this.'

71

Jo nodded. 'He looks as if he's had a hundred fights too many. His poor head!'

Walter faced Peter Bullfinch again. 'Do you understand what a deal is, sir?' he asked politely.

The Ox nodded. His small eyes narrowed. 'A deal is a deal,' he said. 'Don't mess wid me.'

'Well,' said Walter, 'the deal is this. If you can lift that tree above your head, you can have it.'

A look of perfect happiness flooded the Ox's crooked face.

He flexed his arms.

The cannonballs swelled and hardened.

He rose on his toes, tripped lightly over to George, dropped his cudgel, set his legs apart, lowered his torso and gripped George's thigh like a balletic weightlifter.

'Watch this,' he grunted.

George slanted an eye towards Walter, who shook his head imperceptibly. So George lay still, his leg straight and hard as an oak tree.

Peter Bullfinch heaved.

Nothing happened.

'You watching me? You ready? Ooooooh!'

He strained and tugged, but still nothing happened. George did not even blink.

The Ox wiped sweat from his brow. He sniffed. He glanced shiftily at Jo and Walter, who were trying to keep their faces straight, then turned his attention once more to his 'roof tree'.

'C'mon then,' he said, hoping for third-time lucky. 'C'mon, c'mon, c'mon, c'mon, tree. Don't mess wid me, tree. Nobody messes wid Peter Bullfinch. Aaaahhhhh-hhh! Ooooaahhhh-hhh!'

His face contorted and scarlet, the veins standing out like ropes, the Ox hauled with all his might and screamed with the effort he was making. And just when it looked as if he must burst like an overstretched bubble, Walter gave a nod and George kicked his leg in the air.

His knee caught the Ox a crunching blow under the jaw and helped him perform four and a half cartwheels through the leafy glade before landing on his head.

George lowered his leg again.

Jo shrieked helplessly.

Walter choked.

The Ox got up and wandered round in circles. 'I lifted a tree!' he gurgled, to nobody in particular because all he could see were shapes swinging round him in a red mist. 'Nobody messes wid Peter Bullfinch! Now that tree is mine!'

But when he was finally able to stand still and see more clearly, he spotted his cudgel in Walter's hand. 'Thass mine,' he blinked. 'Giz.'

Walter smiled amiably. 'Here's another deal, Mr Bullfinch. If I can make that tree walk, it's mine and I get to keep the cudgel. How's that?'

The Ox tapped the side of his nose wisely. 'You're messin' wid me again,' he sniggered. 'Nobody can make a tree walk.'

'Is it a deal?'

'Or are yous a coward?' purred Jo.

'Deal,' said the Ox sharply. 'C'mon then, c'mon then, make that tree walk.'

Walter crossed to George's leg and waved his arms at it. 'Abracadabra,' he cried in a wailing voice. 'Walk, tree.'

He winked at George and gave a little lift of his head.

Jo prayed that George would understand.

He did.

He flexed his leg.

He raised his knee and drew his foot backwards.

Peter Bullfinch, the toughest man in the world, whimpered. 'Tha's not possible,' he moaned. 'C'mon, stop messin' wid me.' His eyes popped as George's knee rose higher and higher.

Then George flexed his other leg.

'There's two trees!' the Ox yelped, his voice squealing into falsetto. 'No, three!' as George raised his right arm. 'No, four! There's four trees!'

And just as a poacher called Simpkin Sampkins had done two hundred years before when he thought he saw a walking wood, so now Peter Bullfinch fell to his knees and closed his eyes and prayed properly for the first time in his life.

When he opened them again, he saw not just four trees but another one even bigger, and this tree was sitting up, actually sitting up, and it had a face on a pole which leaned down over him and spoke words.

Well, it made noises.

'Grolyhoomp,' it said, in a voice that hummed like the lowest drone of the deepest bagpipe in the world. 'Zwolloqmiddy.'

When Peter Bullfinch, the toughest man in the world, heard a tree play the bagpipes, he fainted clean away.

Chapter Eight
George Builds a House

For more than a year the Ox had been fighting his greatest battle: how to wrestle good land from wasteland.

When he regained consciousness, the bewildered man took Walter, Jo and George to see what he called his 'paradise' – a place where many years ago the forest had given way to marsh and heath and where now, with the Ox's help, that wasteland was being turned into a farm.

In this open space the sun shone unimpeded. The air rang with the songs of different birds to those in the forest. It was here that Peter Bullfinch, a runaway himself, had ploughed and sown, a pioneer setting himself the task of controlling nature.

Day after day, year after year, he had sniffed and

shaken his battered head and grunted, 'C'mon, c'mon, don't mess wid me, ground.'

The results of his labours were a strip of green corn, a patch of grass, a square of straggly vegetables, eight small apple trees and a lot of weeds. Half a dozen sheep were tethered to posts, along with one cow. A couple of pigs snuffled about.

It really did look like a rough little paradise, and Peter Bullfinch was as proud of it as if it had been a kingdom.

'Tha's all mine,' he crowed, waving his arm expansively as they emerged from the trees.

All the livestock, he said, were prizes he'd won by wrestling and boxing at fairs. He would fight for a ram next, and then there would be lambs, and he would have a real farm.

He grinned happily and bounded towards a heap of timbers perched untidily beside the grass, with a tiny heap of rags on top.

'Mudder!' the Ox shouted, 'look who's come to help us!'

He scooped up the rags into his wrestler's arms and bounded back holding them high, as lightly as if they truly had been only rags or feathers.

But they weren't feathers and they weren't quite rags, they were clothes.

Inside them was a hunched little widow woman.

Two black eyes shone like coals deep inside her nut brown face. They glanced sharply at Jo, then at Walter. When they reached Big George they didn't blink, they just stared. She looked about a hundred years old, though probably she was less than sixty.

'Meet my liddle mudder,' Peter Bullfinch said proudly.

'What's that?' asked the widow woman, stabbing a crooked finger towards George.

'Tha's a grolyhoomp, Ma,' Peter Bullfinch whispered. 'Be polite.'

The Ox was totally in awe of George. He nodded towards a tree trunk dangling from George's hand and murmured, 'See that, Ma? He's going to help us wid the house.'

George looked at her. 'Grolyhoomp,' he smiled.

'Humph,' replied the widow woman. She looked as if she'd seen just about everything during her life, and nothing on earth could surprise her now.

The Ox had tried to build one house already, only to have it destroyed by a reckless hunt when it was half complete.

He described how the huntsmen had galloped headlong out of the forest on the trail of a white stag, and had deliberately ridden through the ropes which were holding the house skeleton steady. They had laughed as it tumbled about their horses' heels.

The Ox was determined that his new house would be too strong to be knocked down – if only he could get it finished. He had scoured the forest for perfect timbers, and rough-carved them to the exact shape and size. His brothers were coming to help raise it. The final task had been to find the big sturdy tree that would literally be the house's 'roof tree' – resting on cruck timbers at the ends and centre, it would act like the ridge pole of a tent to make the structure stable and support its roof.

When Peter Bullfinch had revived from his faint and told the others what he was trying to do, they had all searched the forest and finally found a fallen oak which would do the job almost as well as George's leg. And George had happily obliged the Ox by carrying it.

The Ox could hardly believe that something as magical as a grolyhoomp would actually help *him*. He was vociferously grateful.

'Sire, I will be your man,' he sniffed. 'I won't never mess wid you. Anything Peter Bullfinch can do for you, well . . .' he winked and rolled his cannonball muscles, 'you only have to whistle. Know what I mean?'

Then he gave a piercing whistle himself and four young men came running out of the trees.

They were dressed in brightly-coloured smocks of red, blue, purple and green. George beamed at them – especially at the ones in blue and green – and they gazed at him dumbstruck.

The Ox whispered urgently to them, then danced forward. 'Meet my liddle brudders,' he said, with a clumsy attempt at a bow.

Walter returned the bow, Jo tried a curtsey which didn't come off, and George said, 'Ffing-gothrackywok,' meaning, 'How do you do?'

It seemed the Ox's entire family were runaways.

By God's good grace they were still free – though now speechless.

'I've told them not to mess wid him,' Peter Bullfinch told Walter confidentially, 'and not to tell nobody about him neither. Tha's right, isn' it?'

'Dead ri',' said Jo sternly.

'Or else,' said Walter, pointedly gripping the hilt of his sword.

'Can we build the house now?' one of the brothers asked, nodding impatiently at the tree in George's hand.

Thinking they wanted the tree straightaway, George lobbed it casually towards them. They escaped with their lives by a hair's breadth.

Several hectic hours later Ma Bullfinch was stirring a pot over a fire, watched eagerly by the pigs. It bubbled and steamed invitingly.

George, his mouth watering freely at the smell, straddled the new house frame like a colossus. To Walter's frantic signals and the brothers' shouts and the Ox's yelped, 'C'mon now, c'mon now, c'mon, c'mon, c'mon *now*!' he gently lowered the roof tree towards the waiting notches on the three massive crucks.

Jo was running here, there and everywhere, squinting at angles and measuring dimensions with her keen eyes and screaming the results at Walter who, with as much dignity as he could muster – which was very little, because he was extremely excited – conveyed them to George.

George had very little idea of what he was doing or why he was doing it. In fact, ever since he arrived on Earth without bearings or memory, the things he did, good or bad, had happened more or less by accident. But he desperately *wanted* to understand, and he was beginning to feel that one day he might get the hang of some things about this place.

For now, though, helping Walter and Jo get whatever it was they wanted seemed enough of a task. Trying to think beyond it only made his head ache.

But, suddenly, as George stood holding a tree above the heads of yelping midgets, the dream flashed into his mind again.

There was that cold sun.

There were those distant dry mountains.

There again were the fingers playing on the stem of a pipe. But this time the focus stretched to include the hands beyond the fingers – soft hands that moved with extraordinary grace. And for the first time he could hear clearly the sounds they made, a strange and haunting music that disturbed him through and through.

It was so vivid it made George dizzy.

When the midgets saw the roof tree sway and twitch above them, they cried out in alarm. That woke George from his dream.

He blinked, remembered what he'd been doing, and steadied himself. Once more, he followed the movements of Walter's hands, and slowly, slowly, he lowered the roof tree.

George's arm was steady now, and his aim true. And Peter Bullfinch's work was true. The tree fitted snugly into the crucks and the crucks held its weight without breaking or bending or even creaking.

Then ropes were fastened securely to supporting stakes – and the midgets went wild.

The Ox clapped his hands for joy and pirouetted all the way round his skeleton house.

His brothers cheered and held each other's arms and danced.

Ma Bullfinch stirred the pot twice as fast and sang a very weird song in a very cracked voice.

Jo jumped and waved her arms and shouted, 'Yous bleedin' brilliant, Georgie!' and, as a mark of respect, Walter faced the grolyhoomp, drew his sword, pressed the flat of the blade to his forehead and bent his knee.

George laughed. 'Clyyyngissgwodriyn,' he hummed. 'Will that do?'

Now there came the news they had all been waiting for, as little Ma Bullfinch gave a wheeze and a cough and shouted, 'Food!'

That was only the third actual word she'd spoken since they arrived, but it would have been very hard to find a better one.

'C'mon now, c'mon now, don't mess wid Ma's dinner,' cried Peter Bullfinch, who was delighted with the way things were going. 'Who's gunna get it first?'

He raced his brothers to the pot, and Jo and Walter chased after them. But just as George was going to follow, the day blew up like a firework.

A roe deer burst out of the forest. It streaked through the skeleton house, darted under the roof tree, lunged between George's legs and fled through the tiny orchard on to the wide wasteland.

Behind it, with horns blaring, hooves clattering and hounds snapping, a hunt came charging. And for the second time in a week it headed straight for the Ox's half-finished house.

But this time there was a difference.

This time Big George was there.

chapter Nine
what Freedom is

It seemed to George that the day blew apart in an explosion of noise.

First the deer streaked between his feet.

Next a yelping orchestra of hounds of all shapes and sizes poured out of the trees. And after them whirled hunters on snorting horses, men and women in bright array, riding with bows and arrows and spears and unsheathed swords – and two heralds making even more hullaballoo with their horns.

George didn't like the look of the two leading riders. The first leered most unpleasantly and the second slavered freely through bulbous lips. They looked rather nasty. But there was no time for a close examination because they were galloping towards Peter Bullfinch's house.

The entire hunt seemed to be making for the house.

George was at the house.

And this time he did know what he was doing.

To a forty-foot high grolyhoomp they looked like a gang of very noisy dwarves, but George could see that to his new friends they were a disaster.

He saw the Ox race to the front of his home, open wide his arms to protect it and cry like a baby, 'Mudder, they're messin' wid us again!'

He heard the tiny widow woman chirrup like an anguished bird.

He saw her other sons leave their lunch and scatter.

And as for Walter and Jo . . .

Walter knew he was in trouble when he spotted Sir Neville de Magott's coat of arms – a hawk's left foot sticking out of a pudding – emblazoned on a flag held high by one of the heralds. And when he saw that the leading riders were the Maggot himself and his treacherous new steward Jeremiah Wormscrode – the very people who were hunting him as if *he* was a helpless deer – he jumped for cover behind the remains of the pile of timbers and lay flat on the ground with his hands over his head.

And when Nowhere Jo saw the very man *she* was running away from, the man who 'owned' her and

had taken away her home, she spat like an outraged kitten and threw herself down beside Walter.

George experienced their shock like an electric flash in his own mind and moved just as quickly. With astonishing speed for one so big, he crashed down a protective foot in front of the house frame and the babbling Peter. At the same time he opened his lungs, sucked in enough air to empty the atmosphere, lowered his head and blew it out with all his might at the charging hunt.

The hounds didn't like that at all.

One moment, they were yelping with joy at the prospect of tearing a deer to pieces, and the next

they were yowling with fright because they were flying through the air like wingless birds.

The horses didn't like it any better.

The rush of air hit them full on, stopped them in their tracks, and threw them off balance. Whinnying with terror, they reared and tried to bolt.

The riders didn't like that, nor did they like the tornado. They fought to stay in their saddles. They struggled to control their mounts. They battled against panic.

But when one second you're revelling in the thrill of a chase and the next you're flung into a nightmare of flying dogs and howling horses, it jolts you a little. And at that moment the Maggot, the Wormscrode and the others had so much trouble staying seated, they were quite happy to let their horses turn tail on both the freak wind and the Ox, and the house they thought they'd destroyed the week before.

So it was that in the heat of the moment not one of them noticed what caused the hurricane. No one saw Big George.

By the time dusk fell, the house frame was complete and standing sturdily by itself, and Peter Bullfinch was so happy he gave a party.

He built up the fire, and Ma Bullfinch made a broth with vegetables Peter had grown on the land he had wrestled from the wasteland. There was milk from his cow, and a barrel of cider pressed from his own apple harvest. He was so proud he wanted to cry, and when they had all eaten their fill and he had poured more cider, he proposed a toast with tears in his eyes.

'Let's drink to my house,' he sniffed. 'Let's drink to my mudder and my brudders. Let's drink to my friends. And c'mon, let's drink to grolyhoomps!'

At this, his face crumpled so far that his nose crept right inside his bottom lip. But still he hadn't finished. With great dignity, he raised his mug to George and burped, 'Sire, Peter Bullfinch is your man. Any time you need him . . .'

He couldn't go on. He sat down and sobbed.

George's response was to pick up the cider barrel and drain it.

Afterwards, they entertained each other.

The Ox and his brothers performed a tipsy, jumping dance called a saltarello, which ended when they all fell down.

Ma Bullfinch let rip with a peculiar, wailing chant in a voice so hideously cracked nobody could make head or tail of it. But they all applauded and she smiled with toothless pleasure.

Next, Walter stood up in front of the fire, and with a little piping and a lot of acting he told a story he'd once heard a minstrel sing, about a fearless knight who spent his life searching for a magic goblet, only to die the moment he found it.

It was such a miserable story it made everybody depressed, so it was up to Nowhere Jo to cheer them up again.

Jo didn't know how to do it. She was no good at this sort of thing, she said. She was so shy and scared she wanted to run away, but there was nowhere to run to except the forest, and to her surprise she found she didn't want to go back there by herself. She liked it here.

So she said, 'I'll try to do something, all ri'? But it won't be any good.' Then, very nervously, she began a slow, clumsy, hand-clapping and foot-stomping dance, to a gurgling tune she made up as she went along.

It was terrible. She knew it was terrible.

She was so sure it was a ghastly failure, she wanted to die.

But, suddenly, the grolyhoomp started to sway his great head, and clap and hum along with her, and tap his enormous boot, and that gave her more confidence.

Then Walter did the same, and that made

everybody else want to join in, and now Jo found she was getting excited, so she danced faster and faster until she felt she was whirling at a hundred miles an hour, so fast she hardly knew any more which world she was in.

In the end, she too fell down, but her audience clapped and cheered, and even Walter smiled, which made Jo think that at that moment she was happier than she'd been since her ma died. She winked up at George in gratitude, and he winked back.

By now, everybody was looking at George and wondering if grolyhoomps did any entertaining. Could they sing? Could they dance? And if so, would anyone be safe within a mile of those mountainous feet?

Big George answered them in his own way.

It was dark now and starless, and because the fire had burned low, all the light there was came from George's luminous face. It turned their watching faces green, so that it looked as if they were under his spell.

Which, in a way, they must have been, because as George shaped his lips into an O to produce the low bagpipe drone, all their mouths rounded too.

In this way George told them the story of his

dream – of the mountains and the pipe and the fingers, and how these stirred and puzzled him.

Afterwards, he asked if they knew what it meant. But of course he spoke his own language and nobody understood a single word, so they were even more puzzled than he was.

When George tried to explain all over again, the bagpipe drone of his voice was so soothing it sent them into a trance, and long before he had finished, they were all fast asleep.

Jo was woken by rain splashing her face.

It was quite dark and for a moment she couldn't think where she was – she lay on her back, puzzled by the drops and a sound of hissing nearby.

Then she realised that the hissing was raindrops falling onto the glowing embers of the fire, and, in a tumbling rush she remembered the whole amazing day, from waking up a prisoner to falling asleep with a human ox and a snooty boy and a grolyhoomp.

Jo smiled to herself. This was real freedom – wandering at will and having adventures, meeting people and making friends, living for the moment.

She knew it couldn't last. Soon the boy would find his father, the grolyhoomp would head off home – wherever that might be – and she would be caught and returned to the Maggot for some really bad punishment. And that would be the end of that.

Meanwhile, it was raining and a wind was rising.

Walter stirred beside her. 'Are you awake?' he whispered.

'Yiss.'

'It's raining.'

'Yiss.'

'What shall we do?'

'Get wet, unless you've got any ideas.'

Then there came a word like 'Hngusssllossipussoomp', and they felt themselves being lifted and swung gently and laid down again where it was dry and warm. There was a musky smell and they knew they were lying under George. He was better than any house.

'Magic, en't it?' Jo whispered.

'Magic indeed,' said Walter, in the pompous tone that made her want to stick a pin in him.

How different we are, him and me, she thought – and yet, just now we're the same. The law has turned us both into criminals, even though neither of us has done anything wrong. Where's the justice in that? And here we are, sheltering together under the arm of the strangest person either of us has ever seen.

'He's *like* a person, en't he?' Jo whispered. 'George, I mean.'

'He is,' said Walter sleepily. 'But very big.'

'I reckon he's a person, all ri'. But we got to watch out for him, haven't we? I don't trust people.'

'We must honour him.'

'Honner, ri',' said Jo, who hadn't the foggiest notion what the word meant. 'Honner. Yiss, we'll do that.'

She lay still and thought she could hear George's heart beating. 'I like it here,' she said softly.

'So do I,' said Walter. 'Though it would be better without the smell.'

'I think he smells nice.'

'It's not George I'm talking about.'

'I don't smell!'

'Yes you do, you stink, and it's very unpleasant. You're filthy. *And* you have fleas – I've seen you scratching. I expect it's because you live like an animal.'

Jo was outraged. Her cheeks burned and tears scalded her eyes, but they were nothing compared to the fury in her heart. 'I keep myself clean!' she hissed. 'I en't got no fleas and I en't got no smell, all ri'? It was just those men chasin' me into a marsh. That's how they got me – I was sinkin' in mud. They'd never have caught me else.'

'Well, you reek now,' Walter insisted. 'It's disgusting.'

Jo bit her lip and tried to stay silent, but she lost her temper anyway.

'I'll get clean!' she spat. 'Yous watch me, yous stupid knight with your honner! Jus' watch me!'

She scrambled out into the pouring rain. She lifted her face and her arms to it until she was soaked through and streaming. Then she splashed her feet in the puddles and made sure she splashed Walter too, and stamped about, washing her clothes and her body together, all the time cursing the three great banes of her life.

'Drown all damn an' blasted fleas!' she howled. 'Stick all boys in the damn an' blasted pillory! Shove all damn an' blasted lords in the damn an' blasted dungeon!'

Walter kept silent. It seemed best. You have to be careful with wild things, he told himself.

Later, back in her sanctuary, shivering but extraordinarily clean and fresh, Jo heard George quietly going over his latest lesson.

'Damblass,' he muttered softly. 'Damblassimm. Dibdoo.'

By morning the rain was over and gone and the countryside sparkled as freshly as Jo. After Ma Bullfinch had given them breakfast, her son showed them the way they should go through the forest.

'I've been thinking about your da,' the Ox told Walter, 'an' I reckon I seed him three days ago. Meek liddle chap, wouldn't wrestle wid me. He was a Robert.'

The man had been in the company of a band of outlaws who had passed through the Ox's farm on their way to Swineytown, twenty miles away.

The news raised Walter's hopes of finding his father soon, and Jo was delighted by the prospect of going to a town. If she could hide in Swineytown for a year, her troubles might be over.

As they parted, Walter asked Peter Bullfinch not to tell anyone about George. Peter nodded and looked very tough. 'Jus' let anyone try to mess wid my friend,' he growled.

But it isn't easy to keep something as big as a grolyhoomp a secret.

chapter Ten
Some Duck

Jo decided that if she was going to be a free person she had better start acting like one.

That meant learning some manners. The ideal person to teach her was Walter, but she was too proud to ask him. Besides, she knew he would refuse.

So she watched him instead.

She followed Walter about. She listened to him speak. And she copied him. George thought it was a game and followed suit.

It drove Walter crazy.

By the middle of the morning he couldn't stand it another minute. He turned sharply and caught Jo mincing along the track behind him. 'What are you doing?' he snapped.

'Copying yous, Walter, all ri'?' she answered belligerently. 'The way yous walk an' that.'

'You'll never walk like me. You walk like a donkey.'

'An' yous walk like a fish!' Jo cried, wounded sorely. 'I dunno why I want to be like yous!'

Walter drew himself up to his full height – which still left him an inch shorter than Jo – and said haughtily, 'You can never be like me. I shall be a knight. You'll be a scullery maid, if you're lucky.'

'I thought knights had chivalry,' Jo pouted. 'Respect for ladies, an' that.'

Unwisely, Walter gave a sarcastic laugh and sneered, 'Are you trying to tell me you're a *lady*?'

She flew at him then. In an instant, she was on his back, kicking, scratching, biting. Walter yelled. He reached for Jo's hair and yanked her head forward. Then he hooked an arm round her neck and pressed her throat over his collar-bone, choking her.

'Will you yield?' he asked.

'No I wunna,' Jo spluttered, and dug her fingers into his eyes.

In another minute they might have damaged each other, but George intervened.

He took Jo in his left hand, Walter in his right, pulled them apart and dumped them both on the top of his head.

'Ssschhnikkkerthropppy,' he growled, meaning, 'Behave yourselves.'

Then he set off walking, and that was when they really started to travel.

George had had quite enough of dibdoo for the time being, so he braced himself and forged through the forest as if it was a field of flowers. Walter and Jo had to grasp his thick hair to stop themselves falling off. Then they had to get used to the swaying of his long neck. But when they'd achieved that, they found they could look sideways at the sky and down on the birds.

It was like travelling by galloping giraffe.

Big George set his nose in the direction Peter Bullfinch had pointed, and went for it. Leaves swished and branches crashed as he stirred the forest like an enormous spoon. You can imagine how dangerous it was up there on his head. But it was exhilarating too. Walter and Jo peeked at each other through the grolyhoomp's hair, and when they saw their own excitement in each other's eyes, they laughed out loud, all differences forgotten.

This was an experience like no other, and sharing it made them friends at last.

As they journeyed, they crossed streams and bogs and wastes, passing distant fields and villages whose inhabitants shielded their eyes to look at them and then hurriedly crossed themselves as if they'd seen something magical and frightening.

Suddenly, they arrived at a great river.

Beyond the river a rolling line of hills stood up like a rampart against the sky. Clustering below them were the walls and fortifications of a small town.

That had to be Swineytown. They had almost made it.

But to get there they had to cross the river.

In those days it was easier and cheaper to travel by river than by road, and the water in front of them was busy with boats, some ferrying passengers, others transporting farm produce, logs and coal.

There were barges with oars, barges with sails, rowing boats, sailing boats and wherries. Heavy horses plodded along each bank, hauling flat-bottomed towboats.

To Jo and Walter, who had never seen a river as big as this, it looked bewildering. To George it seemed as if the entire surface of the water was in motion.

He saw he would have to be careful where he put his feet or he would sink a dozen craft. Even so, as he waded in he caused dangerous waves and the nearby boats rocked crazily.

When they saw George enter the river, the steersmen forgot their tillers and the sailors their sails.

Horses bolted and their towboats dived.

Captains collapsed, crews cringed, and craft collided and capsized.

In no time, the swirling river was littered with upturned boats and swimmers desperately fleeing the monster.

The river was deep. After three steps the water was up to George's chest. Two more and it lapped his beard.

'Do yous reckon Georgie can swim?' asked Jo.

'I hope he can, because I can't,' Walter replied faintly.

Jo thought he looked rather blue about the mouth, and gave him a look which said, 'That's one more useless thing about yous, knight or no knight,' but before she could say it, George stepped into a hole and the water came over his head.

If Walter had stayed calm he might have floated. But he didn't stay calm. He panicked.

He yelled.

He punched the water with his fists as if he would beat it into submission.

When that didn't work, he sank.

But when he came up again, spluttering and still thrashing, Jo was ready for him. She swam up close, trod water and whacked him across the face.

That surprised Walter so much that he stopped punching long enough for Jo to cup his head in her arms and turn over on her back and float, cradling him.

'Yous struggle one more time an' I'll scratch your eyes out,' she panted. 'After that I'll push yous down, all ri'?'

Walter kept still.

As for George, when he first went under he was as shocked as Walter. This was another new experience for him. He'd never drowned before.

The dry mountains swam through his mind, and the fingers moved across his water-filled eyes, and the music of the pipe mingled in his ears with the bubbling rush of the river. It was very strange and beautiful, but George knew that it was also dangerous.

Then he too bounced back to the surface. He felt the sun on his face and the water buoying him up, and suddenly he found he was swimming – clumsily and with a great deal of splashing, but swimming.

George loved it. He paddled about like a duck on a pond. The effect on the river was awesome. Huge waves surged in all directions, toppling more boats and turning sobbing swimmers into screaming surfers. Fish were flung into the air, and Jo and Walter rose and sank and rose and sank until they were seasick.

'Don't let go of me!' Walter cried.

Jo frowned. 'Are yous sorry for what yous said about me?'

'Yes!'

'Say it, then.'

'I'm sorry! I'll never insult you again!'

'And I'm a lady, en't I? Tell me I'm a lady.'

Walter ground his teeth. It cost him a lot of effort, but finally he gasped, 'Yes, you are. You're a lady.'

Jo smiled. Lady Joanne – of Somewhere. It had been worth falling in the river just to hear this snooty knight-apprentice say that.

'Georgie!' she shouted. 'Will yous stop messing about and help us, all ri'?'

chapter Eleven
The End of the world

The watchman on the tower could not believe what he was seeing. He shaded his eyes and scanned eastward a second time, towards the distant river.

This is what he thought he saw.

He thought he saw tidal waves sweeping up, down and across it, although he knew the river had no tide.

He thought he saw all the river craft overturn and their passengers dive into the water as if a hurricane had capsized them, although he could feel there was no wind.

He thought he saw a head the size of several bulls forging through the water, although everybody knows there is no head as big as that.

Therefore, since everything the watchman saw

was impossible, he didn't believe his eyes.

Then, it seemed to him that the head reached the near bank and rose up above it like a pomegranate on a pole.

He didn't believe that, either.

'I'm not cut out for this job,' he thought. 'I get visions.'

For comfort, the watchman looked away, left and right along the town walls. They looked solid enough, thank goodness, and free of mirages. He relaxed a little.

Then he glanced down on his home town. All four gates – north, south, east and west – were wide open for market day, and Swineytown's narrow streets of painted houses bustled with stalls, traders, merchants, pedlars and all manner of town and country folk. Bright shop signs above their heads flashed in the sun. Craftsmen worked inside, making shoes, forging metal, stitching leather, while outside drovers herded cattle, sheep, pigs and geese as best they could through the winding lanes.

It was chaos, but it was always chaos and the watchman loved it. It also stank, but that too was normal.

The watchman's name was Martin, of Watery Lane, Swineytown. He was a short man, square-

bodied, square-headed and square-faced, and he was bowed down with worry.

'It's all very well for our burgesses to say every man must take his turn at being a policeman,' he muttered, 'but I'm a citizen, not a soldier. I'm a butcher, not a constable. They shouldn't put a man like me on duty up here. I can't guard the town. I'm a coward. And I see things.'

He stole another uneasy glance eastward, and this time he saw the pomegranate head floating above the wood that stretched from the river to the town.

'My dad's bottom on it but I'm a sick man,' he moaned.

Then he turned his back on the vision and hurried to tell his Swineytown comrades what he thought he had seen, but of course didn't believe.

Thirty minutes later, Walter and Jo left George lying low among the trees and entered the east gate of Swineytown, in search of news, money and food.

Walter intended to earn money as a travelling minstrel. Jo planned to pick up a few tasty things from the produce stalls.

They would both keep their ears open for news of outlaws and Walter's father.

Jo set out to steal, and on a vacant corner just off the town square, Walter turned himself into a one-boy travelling band. He played his three-hole pipe with his right hand, hit his tabor drum with his left and stamped the ground rhythmically with each foot in turn and sometimes both together.

He was good. He had practised hard at his music lessons, and before long the nearby traders were twitching and tapping their feet. While they were thus happily occupied, Jo picked their pockets.

She was good at that.

Coins were thrown into the cap Walter had placed on the ground beside him. That encouraged a hunchbacked hurdy-gurdy player to join him. Then a stick-thin fiddler arrived. Together they played a jolly saltarello and the market folk hooked arms and jumped up and down the street.

That was a sight to see!

But there was more than people jigging.

There was a bear dancing at the end of a chain.

There was a little dog capering in circles.

And outside the town wall there was Big George.

George liked music. He found its rhythms irresistible. When he heard the jumping dance he gave up lying low, looked over the wall to see what was going on, and pranced about.

When the townspeople saw him, they knew they should be frightened, because according to the rumours, George was probably the beginning of the end of the world. But his glowing, blue-green, hairy pomegranate of a face looked so funny jiggling about up there on its long neck that they laughed instead.

Now, when a crowd of people starts to laugh at somebody because they think he looks odd, it can sometimes turn nasty.

It turned nasty now.

Soon, instead of laughing at George the people of Swineytown were mocking him, and instead of dancing they were taunting, and instead of singing they were jeering. Then they began to throw things at George. Eggs, for instance, and overripe turnips.

Jo and Walter were dismayed. Walter bagged his takings and Jo stole a sack to carry hers, but just when they were ready to run to George, matters grew even worse.

The little capering dog caught the crowd's change of mood and, suddenly, instead of dancing with the bear, he began baiting it.

Other dogs, hearing the rumpus, came yapping and joined in.

The bear's master tried to keep them at bay, but there were too many of them. Then the bear herself became worried, because here were all these dogs jumping at her, snarling and biting, but she couldn't fight back because she was chained to a wall.

She didn't like that.

Neither did Jo, who screamed, nor Walter.

Neither did George.

Three things happened almost together.

First, some people joined the dogs and started baiting the bear as well as the grolyhoomp.

That caused the bear to yank her chain right out of the wall and begin lashing out to defend herself.

And George jumped over the town wall.

When he landed inside, he flattened fourteen market stalls and scattered forty-six pigs, twenty-one cows, thirty-seven sheep and about five hundred geese. Rejoicing in their unexpected freedom they all ran grunting, mooing, baaing and honking through the twisting streets of Swineytown at what seemed about ninety miles an hour.

At first, the folk thought George had come to help them fight the bear, so they cheered him.

But when they realised it was the other way round – which was quite soon because George started protecting the bear by flicking its attackers with his fingers, left and right up the street – he became Public Enemy Number One.

It was pandemonium. The noise was eardrum-shattering, especially when, on top of everything else, George began chuntering 'grolyhoomp' and 'dammblassimm'.

A worried little man with a square head ran into the square. He nudged Jo and muttered, 'This is a proper horse's bottom, isn't it? G-god preserve me from giant pomegranates. But none of it is real, you know. It's just me, seeing things. I'm going to lie down for a bit and then everything will be all right.'

He backed away, wistful and wincing, into the doorway of a butcher's shop, and disappeared.

Then, out of the blue, a fourth thing happened.

Swineytown was invaded.

The first anybody knew of this was when two fat trumpeters staggered into the square and blew a strangled fanfare, which frightened the birds. Behind them, a red-cheeked town crier came puffing and bellowing, 'Oyez! Muster-at-arms! Muster-at-arms! Brigands ahorse! Oyez!'

The result of his announcement was immediate, universal, heart-stopping panic.

Even the dogs took fright and ran away.

The townspeople forgot about the bear.

They forgot about Big George.

They had only two thoughts in their heads – how to preserve their property and their lives. In that order.

George, Jo, Walter and the bear were amazed. They had never seen anything disappear so fast. One minute the streets were stuffed with produce and livestock and the next it was flying into attics, tumbling into cellars and stampeding along dark alleyways.

Windows closed, doors banged shut, and the square and the streets were empty. It was like a conjuring trick.

Swineytown became a ghost town.

George and his friends gazed around in the silence, bewildered and quite alone.

But they weren't alone for long. Somebody was about, somewhere. They heard the sound of tramping feet.

It grew louder and marching into the square there came the most ragged troop of troops you ever saw.

You wouldn't call them soldiers.

They couldn't even pretend to be soldiers.

They were citizens of Swineytown – a ramshackle brigade of shopkeepers, street sweepers, cord-wainers, manure pickers and heaven knows what else. Between them they carried some bows and arrows and a few clubs and staves. They all looked very, very frightened.

When they saw Big George they quailed.

'He won't hurt you,' Walter told them. 'He's a grolyhoomp.'

They didn't seem to find that very reassuring.

'He's a friend, all ri'?' said Jo. 'En't yous, Georgie?'

'Dammblassimm,' George said.

The recruits rolled their eyes, but eventually focused on the butcher's shop from which Citizen Martin was emerging, hastily arranging his tunic

and carrying a sword three sizes too big for him.

When he reached the troop he cried, 'Attenshun! Hands up who has the keys to the town gates!'

Nobody moved.

Citizen Martin cleared his throat. 'Hands up who *shut* the gates!'

Still, nobody moved. The troops looked shiftily at each other.

As the implication sank in, Martin's eyes opened very wide. *Nobody* had shut the gates.

His hair stood on end.

Then he looked George straight in the eye, as if grolyhoomping pomegranates were the least of his problems, cupped his hands to his ears – and heard what he dreaded to hear.

George heard it too, and the troops heard it and Jo and Walter heard it and the bear heard it.

They all heard galloping hooves entering the town.

chapter Twelve
Three and a Bear

In the Year of Our Lord 1305 gangs of brigands, often in the pay of powerful lords, roamed the countryside, plundering manor houses, churches, villages and even towns.

The gang approaching Swineytown numbered fifty leather-jacketed men armed with bows, swords, spears, flails, hooks, knives, crowbars and pickaxes. Thundering along on their half-wild horses they were a terrifying sight.

It was rumoured that they were being paid by Jeremiah Wormscrode, steward to Sir Neville de Magott, to punish Swineytown because its citizens had refused to pay him protection money.

Walter could believe that.

Jo could believe that.

Whatever their motive, the brigands rode

headlong through the open west gate and began to lay the town waste, smashing, looting, burning – and terrorising anyone they came across. Every troop of citizens sent to stop them had fled at the first sight of their slashing swords, and now only Citizen Martin's militia, shaking in their pointed shoes, stood in their way.

When Martin heard the hooves enter Watery Lane he closed his eyes and whimpered. In a few seconds they would mow him down, and his friends with him.

He closed his eyes.

'Lord,' he prayed frantically, 'I am a simple man and no doubt unworthy of favours, but would you be so kind as to send me a miracle, please?'

He begged so hard it hurt, then opened his eyes expecting to see spears and flails and pickaxes come sweeping round the corner into the square.

Instead, he saw Big George, and Martin the Swineytown butcher knew that his prayer had been answered before he'd even asked it.

The grolyhoomp was his miracle.

What happened next was another miracle: the brigands failed to arrive. They never emerged from Watery Lane.

This was how it came about.

Walter and Jo, realising they were in even more

danger from Jeremiah Wormscrode's villains than the citizens of Swineytown, stepped forward to join Martin's militia and fight with them side by side.

That stirred Big George.

When he saw their courage he decided to help.

He stepped over their heads and planted his boot in the entrance to Watery Lane and blocked it.

The lane was just wide enough for horsemen to ride up it two abreast. That suited George perfectly. As the thieves and murderers came jangling and clattering he dipped down like a heron after fish and snatched them up a pair at a time – right hand, left hand, right hand, left hand – and tossed them over his shoulder, over the walls and out of the town.

Each brace of brigands saw the Hands of Justice swoop down from the sky. Each felt themselves collected and crunched, then flung and flying, and they all knew without the shadow of a doubt that at last they were getting their just desserts.

Twenty-four pairs of villains soared like that. The twenty-fifth pair had time to turn around and ride like the wind the other way.

Unfortunately for them, they weren't fast enough.

George reached down and snatched them up. Like a man throwing a discus he swung his arm wide and flung them high and far, far and high, spinning them into a huge looping arc that carried them to the very middle of the river, where they sank three rowing boats and a wherry.

Watching these last villains leave his beloved town so spectacularly made little square Martin smile for the first time that day.

'Martin,' he told himself, 'you may be a simple man, and you may be a coward, but you have amazing visions.'

So Big George was transformed from End of the World and Public Enemy Number One to the Saviour of Swineytown inside a few exciting minutes.

'These midgets are very changeable,' he observed, as citizens tumbled from their houses and ran rings round his legs. 'But I suppose it makes life interesting.'

Walter was still no closer to finding his father. But that night they had a piece of luck.

As afternoon moved into evening, the townspeople brought them food by the cartload and fêted them merrily. There was dancing. George capered a jig and Walter even measured some elegant steps with Jo, who managed not to fall over and, for a few minutes, felt almost a lady.

At sundown the gates were locked. Bells sounded a curfew to warn everybody to go home, because there were no street lights and it was dangerous to be out after dark.

One by one, the citizens returned to their homes, and soon Walter, Jo and George were left alone again.

They decided to spend the night in the square, because that was the only space big enough for George to lie down in.

It was very smelly, since an open drain ran through it, but Walter and Jo were used to stink and George accepted it as just one more peculiar custom of this constantly surprising world.

They lay side by side on the ground and watched dusk turn to darkness. The only light now came from George's face and the dim tallow candles flickering inside the windows of the houses. Soon even those were snuffed out.

There were noises – owls, and cats, and rats that skittered past their feet and plopped into the drain. And there was another, quite different sound – the chink of a dragging chain.

The bear was still around.

At a loss without her master, who had fled from the town when the tumult was at its height, she was creeping close to the people who had befriended her.

Walter wasn't sure he liked that. He grabbed a handful of pebbles and threw them at the noise. 'Scat!' he shouted.

'No!' cried Jo. 'Let her come.'

'Why?'

'Because I want her, all ri'?'

Jo fumbled round the square until she heard the bear's breathing, then felt for the chain and gave it a tug.

The bear came willingly.

'I'll chase it while you're asleep,' Walter warned her.

'Yous can say goodbye to your eyes, then.'

'Zwifnnbwww,' said George. 'Let the bear come.'

Even in the dark George had felt Jo's longing, and he realised that behind the tough exterior that was her defence against a dangerous world, there hid a lonely girl who wanted a friend above all else.

Now, once again, they lay quiet.

Jo ruffled the bear's dirty fur and sighed contentedly. 'Now we're four outlaws, en't we?' she whispered.

'I'm leader,' Walter said arrogantly.

'No you en't. Nobody's leader. We're all equal.'

'*You're* my equal?' gasped Walter, trembling with indignation.

'Yiss, I am.'

'And the bear, I suppose? The bear is my equal, too?'

'Yiss.'

'And the grolyhoomp?'

'The grolyhoomp most of all. He's more equal than any of us.'

Walter knew she was right.

While his friends bickered, George – who was

used to one day lasting nine hundred earthly years – was trying to come to terms with a world where night seemed to fall with every blink of an eye.

And he was listening to the stars.

Why did it always seem as if they were speaking to him? What were they saying? He lay on his back in the little walled town, watching galaxies spin overhead, and he heard their song like wind lyres.

'Gardey-loo! Gardey-loo!' cried a woman's voice, as she emptied a chamber pot out of a window. The splash echoed round the square, and a surprised and sodden cat ran scampering down Watery Lane.

Then a timid voice whispered, 'Who g-goes there?', and a candle lantern wavered into view, shaking nervously in the hand of the Swineytown nightwatchman.

He stopped at the edge of the pitch-black square. 'Does *anybody* go there?' he croaked. 'Show yourselves if you do.' He raised the lantern but all it illuminated was his own face – the haunted face of Citizen Martin carrying out his last duty of the day.

'Grolyhoomp,' George said.

Martin nearly dropped his lantern. He peered towards a ghostly green glimmer in the middle of the square. From where he was standing it looked like the biggest glow-worm in creation.

'Is that you, my miracle?' he breathed. 'Are you still there?'

Jo said, 'We're all here. Why don't yous come and join us?'

Martin did – and changed the course of their quest.

Sitting down beside them, he ventured his opinion that life was a pig's bottom. He might be only a simple man but he knew which side his bread was buttered, and that was his bedside. He'd be relieved to find himself there alive and well when his spell of guard duty was over, because it would be a lot more than the previous nightwatchman had managed.

'Why, what happened to him?' Walter asked sleepily.

'Master Wormscrode's spies cut his throat, boy.'

'Why did they do that?'

Martin explained that only yesterday morning a handful of outlaws had arrived in Swineytown, bringing with them a gentleman who asked for the town's protection. It was granted, and the outlaws left without harming anybody, but just before sundown a trio of thoroughly nasty-looking men had slipped into town and concealed themselves until dark.

During the night they came out of hiding,

kidnapped the gentleman and escaped with him over the town wall.

The nightwatchman must have disturbed them. He would never disturb anybody else again.

It was Martin's opinion that this afternoon's raid was a revenge attack upon Swiney for harbouring the gentleman.

It was typical of Jeremiah Wormscrode, who was a bad man to cross.

'What was the gentleman's name?' asked Walter, wide awake now.

'Robert,' Martin answered. 'His name was Robert. Poor man, I wouldn't give a snail's bottom for his chances now.'

chapter Thirteen
Trial by combat

They left Swineytown as soon as its gates were opened in the morning.

Walter's heart was heavy, for he knew he was returning to what was for him the most dangerous place in the world – Sir Neville de Magott's castle.

It was the worst possible place for Jo, too.

She had lain awake most of the night, wondering what she should do. The thought of leaving the town on which all her hopes of freedom rested, only hours after setting foot in it, horrified her. Why, even to think about it would have been impossible for her a week ago.

But Jo was changing.

It was when she saw the gates opening that she finally made up her mind. There and then she cast all doubts aside, collected the bear's chain and led her out of town.

Walter was astounded.

'You know what will happen if you're caught,' he said, 'so why take the risk?'

Jo shrugged. 'Because it's like family, all ri'?'

'What do you mean?'

'Georgie an' yous an' the bear – you're all there is for me. I en't got nobody else. Anyhow, who's gunna hold your head up when yous fall in a river again?'

There was no answer to that.

It seemed that their quest was going to end where it began, and that thought cast a gloom over Walter and Jo as they headed back towards Magotty Castle.

George felt their anxiety as if it was his own. He was finding that the longer he was in their company, the more he was becoming involved with their destiny. So he stayed close by them and walked dibdoo so he wouldn't give them away.

For their part, Jo and Walter kept watch for hunters who might be tempted to attack a grolyhoomp from the cover of the trees, thinking him the biggest and best game they had even seen.

In this way they guarded each other and hid from everybody else.

On the second day they met a caravan lumbering through the forest. George held the bear's muzzle to keep her quiet, while Walter and Jo watched the passing cavalcade with growing dismay.

It was like a circus.

A dozen wagons swayed along the uneven track, laden with the belongings of several knights and their ladies and household retinues. They had dogs and donkeys and goats with them, and pilgrims and other travellers had tagged themselves on the end, deeming it wise to band together for safety and company in the dangerous forest.

The bright colours of their clothes, the painted wagons and the horses' flashing harness made such a show that George's heart leaped to see them. But they threw Walter into deep gloom.

'They're heading for Magotty Castle for the midsummer festival and tournament,' he said. 'I'd forgotten about it. There will be cavalcades like this all over the forest, and that means the castle and all the land around it will be full to bursting. How can I rescue my father with all those people everywhere?'

He had vaguely hoped to find out where his dad was being held prisoner, and somehow sneak him out when nobody was looking. That plan was now in ruins.

'Don't worry, there'll be a way,' Jo said confidently, to cheer him. 'We'll just have to find it, all ri'?'

Walter nodded, but there were tears in his eyes.

Sure enough, when they reached the edge of the forest and looked out towards the hill on which Magotty Castle stood, they saw an amazing sight.

All the land around the base of the hill was crammed with rainbow-coloured pavilions. It looked like the encampment of a great army the night before a battle, except that this camp was thronged with people singing, dancing, shouting, eating, drinking and playing games.

Over it all loomed the whitewashed walls, painted roof and fluttering banners of Magotty Castle, glinting majestically on its green hill like a palace in a fairy tale.

George was entranced. 'Zzynnymmroggleth-wingerotygon!' he breathed. 'Will you take a look at that, now!'

Walter winced. It didn't look entrancing to him, it looked impossible. All he saw was crowded tents and watchmen pacing the castle battlements, and he knew he could never slip past all those without being noticed.

The alternative – to push boldly through the

middle of it all as though he had every right to be there – was too terrifying to think about. So Walter didn't think about it. He did it.

Telling Jo, George and the bear to wait for him under cover of the trees, he stepped out into bright sunshine and a world of midsummer madness.

Then, taking a deep breath to still his thudding heart, Walter walked steadily forward, into the lions' den.

Inside the fairy castle the fairy king was strutting round and round his great hall, congratulating himself.

'What an amazing man I am!' he chortled. 'What intellect I possess! What brilliance! What power of thought! Who else would even dream of staging a public execution to round off a midsummer festival, eh, Wormscrode? It's genius, that's what it is. I'm surprised there's room for my mind in my head – eh, what?'

'To be sure, sire,' sniggered the toady scurrying behind him, 'you have the brain of the century. And I'm the man to tell you so, to be sure.'

Sir Neville de Magott leered stiffly at his new steward. He was a strange-looking man, tall, thin and rigid – picture a cardboard rectangle with a head and you've got him. But the oddest thing about him was his leer.

Sir Neville leered all the time. He never stopped. He leered when he smiled, when he frowned and when he was furious. He leered at breakfast, lunch and dinner. He woke up leering and went to sleep leering into his pillow. He even leered in his dreams.

This gave an odd twist to his face, a sideways expression that was downright unpleasant. It was particularly unpleasant just now.

Jeremiah Wormscrode, with his cringing manner, drooling mouth and thin, trailing moustache that looked like a slug on a wet cushion, was no pin-up either.

Jeremiah had risen in the world by aping the moods of his masters. When they smiled, he smiled. When they were angry, he was angry too. When they cried, he cried, and if they made a joke, he roared his head off. That lulled them into thinking they had the perfect servant, at which point Jeremiah betrayed them and took over their position.

He had done that to the trusting, honourable Robert of Swyre, and now here he was in the Great Hall as Sir Neville's right-hand man, while Robert was down in the dungeon.

So it was that when Walter was catapulted into the hall by the castle guards, he was greeted by the two people he most dreaded to meet.

The Maggot was delighted to see him.

'Look who's here, Wormscrode,' he crowed. 'Come to see his dad, I expect.'

'I have, sir,' said Walter, trying hard to be brave, 'and also to plead for mercy. I beg you to spare the life of Robert of Swyre and grant him a pardon.'

'Beg pardon?'

Sir Neville's leer assumed a new character,

outraged and menacing. 'You're asking me to be merciful to a traitor? And to yourself, too, I suppose – you'll be wanting *two* pardons, forsooth. You've got a hope.'

The Maggot jerked about dramatically and waved stiff arms as if he'd been starched from head to foot. 'I'll tell you what you *will* get, Walter of Swyre,' he snorted, 'you'll get a double beheading. At sundown on Midsummer Night, as the climax to the jousting, you and your dad can say hello to the axe. How does that sound? He-he-he, another smart idea, eh, Wormscrode?'

'He-he-he, to be sure, sire,' Jeremiah simpered.

Walter felt his face turn pale and his legs tremble. But he stood his ground, kept his head and thought fast – faster even than the Maggot.

'You mentioned jousting, sir,' he said carefully. 'Would you agree to include in it a trial by combat for my father's life?'

'Trial by combat?' Sir Neville squeaked.

'Trial by combat?' squealed Jeremiah. 'Whose trial, boy? Whose combat?'

Walter was inspired. Very politely, he reminded Sir Neville of an ancient custom which allowed a man accused of a crime to try to prove his innocence by challenging his accuser to a duel.

Looking hard at Jeremiah Wormscrode, he

added, 'If my lord will permit, I will take part in the tournament and fight for my father's life. If I win it, he is innocent and goes free. How does that sound?'

For a moment, the Maggot was speechless. Then he roared with laughter and slapped his wooden knees.

The Wormscrode smiled half-heartedly.

'By gad, you've got a nerve, boy,' Sir Neville chortled. 'You're hardly big enough to get on a horse, let alone do battle from it, yet you think you can joust with my best knights at the tourney *and win*?'

'I will fight them for my father's life,' Walter doggedly repeated. He was standing very straight now, and though his face was pale, his eyes were shining.

'What a lark,' said the Maggot gleefully. 'Two entertainments for the price of one! We'll have a battle between a puny David and a cartload of Goliaths – and almost certainly a death when he gets his block knocked off – and we'll *still* have our execution at the end! That can't be bad, eh, Wormscrode?'

'Sire,' protested Jeremiah, 'you cannot be serious—'

Sir Neville slapped him soundly about the ears. 'Don't you *sire* me,' he said, leering harder and

wider than ever. 'I'm the genius around here. What I say, goes. But . . .' here he hesitated and frowned '. . . if I am the genius, why didn't I have that idea? Why didn't *you*, you idiot? Why'd you leave it to a boy? Where's the use in a steward without an intelligent thought in his head? And what are you grinning at? You're always grinning, Wormscrode, I've noticed.'

He battered Jeremiah's ears all the way up the great hall and back again.

When he returned, breathless with the exertion, the Maggot told Walter, 'You have two days to prepare yourself, boy. Tomorrow is Midsummer Eve and the tourney is the day after. That isn't long, so you'd better get practising. We want a good show. And hear this – when you ride into the lists you'll be entering a knockdown tournament. You must win every round, so that by the end you're the only one left sitting on a horse. Otherwise, you die and your father dies. Have you got that?'

Walter blinked. 'Yes, my lord.'

'Very well. Go and get yourself kitted out. Wormscrode, fix him up with a horse and armour and a shield and a lance and anything else he needs. And fix yourself up while you're about it, because if by some miracle this boy gets past the others, you'll be his last obstacle. That's fair, since you were his father's accuser.'

When he heard this Jeremiah Wormscrode gave such a triumphantly evil leer of his own, you would think he'd been practising it all his treacherous life, just for this moment.

'Dismiss,' said the Maggot to both of them. 'And may the bravest man win.'

Walter was brave enough now to dare one last request. Unfortunately, it was one too many.

'Please, sir, may I see my father?'

Sir Neville de Magott shook his creaking head like the pendulum of a rusty clock. 'You may not,' he tocked. 'But you *will* see him, boy. And he will see you. On Midsummer Day I promise he'll have the best seat at the tourney, to watch you die.'

chapter fourteen
Bring On the Dancing Knights

'**Y**mmylllochmidjoo?' asked Big George, meaning, 'What's that, Jo?'

From their shelter among the trees, George, Jo and the bear had seen the midsummer gathering grow ever bigger as they watched anxiously for Walter's return. Now, Jo squinted along George's pointing finger and saw, through a tiny gap among the pavilions, some peasants raising a rough wooden structure at the foot of castle hill.

Two long lines of board enclosed a strip of green like a race track. Beyond them, a bank of seating rose high in the air.

'Those are the lists, Georgie,' Jo explained.

'Ll-iss-tss?'

'For the jousting, all ri'?'

'Jjowwwsstngg.'

'That's the word. But oh, Georgie, I wish we didn't have to hide all the time, don't yous? I wish we could just go out there, ri', and enjoy the fair, and walk about and not be afraid. Just be free.'

'Fff-rr-eeee.'

'It's good to belong to somebody, like your family – but without bein' *owned*, ri'? The law says I'm the Maggot's property, and I can't stand that. Georgie, what d'yous think is going to happen to me? And what's going to happen to yous? If yous was to go out there they'd use yous for target practice. On top of that yous can't even speak sense – well, not so anybody can understand, anyway.'

She looked at him with troubled eyes. George gave her a wide, gentle smile. 'Grolyhoompjoo,' he said softly.

Jo grinned. 'That's your answer to everything, en't it? Well, maybe it's not a bad one. Hello then, what's this?'

She pointed at a mysterious object lumbering through the tents towards them. It looked like a mobile scrap heap.

As it came closer they heard clanking sounds and saw underneath the scrap a bony, dejected-looking grey horse, and behind it all a red-faced boy who

146

kept prodding the horse with a warped lance to keep it moving.

The boy was Walter, the nag his fiery steed, and the bits of rusty tin and mesh were his armour for the tournament. These, and the bent and splintered lance, were all that Sir Neville's miserable, mean, sly steward had allowed him.

'How can I possibly joust some of the best knights in the kingdom with this lot?' Walter groaned, as he told them the Maggot's edict. 'I'll never survive the first round, let alone win the tourney and save my dad's life. They plan to execute him as the climax to the festival!'

'Why did yous volunteer?' asked Jo, looking puzzled.

Walter sighed. 'Because I couldn't think of anything else. And because I was good at jousting in my knight accomplishment classes. But that was kid's stuff, played for fun. This will be the real thing, and deadly serious.'

Jo looked at his pale, grave face and in her mind's eye saw him hobbling into the lists. 'Don't worry,' she said brightly, 'there probably won't even be a contest. Because one look at yous an' those real knights will fall off their horses laughing.'

All day long a constant stream of cavalcades like the one they had met in the forest toiled up the hill to the castle, bringing new knights and their families to the festival.

Among them Walter saw the dreaded black eagle banner of Sir Ribrub de Crackling and his son

Ralph. Sir Ribrub, the Dark Knight, was last year's jousting champion and a favourite to win again – which meant that if Walter survived the early rounds he would almost certainly come up against him in the lists.

That was a most unpleasant prospect.

As well as the great knights who owned vast estates, many knights who had no land at all had also been drawn to the tourney in the hope of winning a big prize. Most of them were poor and shabby and looked, like Peter Bullfinch, rather beaten about the edges.

It so happened that the poorest, shabbiest and most beaten knight in the land was at that moment being beaten again in a faded green pavilion not a hundred feet from where George and his friends were hiding.

His name was Sir Harry le Frit, and his assailant was his sister Gwendolyn.

'Get out of my sight, you big booby!' Gwendolyn bellowed in a deep roar that was anything but ladylike. 'Go out there and fight for us!'

The pavilion doorflap billowed open and a tin scarecrow hurtled out and fell flat on his back. A helmet followed.

Inside the pavilion the voice ranted, 'Find

another idiot to practise with – heaven knows you need it!'

'Yes, Gwenny dear, I will, right away, dear,' the scarecrow muttered, collecting the helmet and struggling to his feet with a lot of creaking and grinding.

Once upright, he looked directly towards the trees and spotted Walter sorting his scrap. He clanked over.

When he saw Walter he said, 'That was my sister Gwen. Isn't she sweet? She wants me to win the tourney.' At that his face fell and his pale blue eyes looked as though they could weep. 'But I've never won anything in my life and I don't see how I'm going to start now. One look at a lance and I'll be flat on my back, as usual.'

'Same here,' said Walter.

'The trouble is,' the scarecrow continued, 'I don't like hurting people – though I've noticed they don't mind hurting me. Gwen says if there was a booby prize for the tallest and most incompetent knight, I'd win it every time.'

'If there was a prize for the smallest and most stupid of knights, I'm sure I'd win it,' said Walter sympathetically.

The scarecrow smiled, bowed and held out a thin, mailed fist. 'Sir Harry le Frit, at your service.'

'Walter of Swyre, at yours, sir,' said Walter, shaking the fist.

'Jo of Nowhere,' said Jo, shaking it also.

'I'm not really a *sir* at all,' their new friend admitted, 'or even a *le*. I just call myself that because it sounds imposing. It doesn't make a groat of difference, though. I still get beaten.'

Sir Harry le Frit put on his helmet, tried to look fierce – and noticed George.

His breathing accelerated inside his helmet. Steam seeped through the slits in his visor.

'Wh-wh-wh-whatever is *that*?' he panted.

'*That*,' said Jo and Walter together, very firmly, 'is our secret. Now he's yours, too.'

Within a few minutes they had negotiated a deal whereby, in return for George not sitting on him, Sir Harry would keep his mouth shut. He would also help Walter prepare for the tourney by giving him the benefit of his long – though each time short lived – experience.

'If you remember that nothing I do ever works,' he said brightly, 'and therefore do the opposite of whatever I tell you, you can't go wrong.'

While Walter was trying to work this out, Jo finally lost patience with hiding. Announcing that, 'There's no point in being free if you can't do what you want,' she followed Walter's example and stepped boldly out of the trees into the excitement of the midsummer festival, disguised as a roving entertainer, with her cap jammed down across her eyes and a bear dancing behind her at the end of a rope.

An hour later she was arrested.

But what an hour that was!

The bear danced and Jo jigged, and as they spun a corkscrew trail through the bright pavilions, people clapped and threw money.

They bumped continually into other entertainers – strolling players, musicians, acrobats and jugglers, all making a loud noise to draw attention to themselves. They passed stalls selling ale and trinkets and pies. They dodged gamblers playing games with dice and drunks rolling about singing.

Jo felt dizzy with the excitement of it all.

Then, right in the middle of the pavilions they came upon a wrestling ring. Inside it there danced a man as big as an ox, who flexed his cannonball muscles and sniffed as he pirouetted on his toes and heaved all comers over the ropes into oblivion.

'C'mon now, c'mon now, c'mon now,' Peter Bullfinch challenged the onlookers, 'who's next?'

Jo sent in the bear.

'Don't mess wid me!' the Ox cried, sticking up his fists, but when he saw Jo he laughed and jumped down and tossed her into the air. 'Jo!' he cried happily, 'my liddle friend! What you doin' here?'

When she explained, the Ox tutted and his battered face looked thoughtful, but then he grinned and said, 'Tell Walter not to worry. The strongest man in the world will come to the tourney.'

Jo moved on through the fair, wondering what a dancing wrestler could do against armoured knights on horseback.

She was still thinking about it when she turned a corner and found herself staring into the thick-lipped, slavering face of Jeremiah Wormscrode.

'You and that bear,' he slurped, 'are under arrest.'

When Jo was brought before Sir Neville de Magott, an enormous banquet was taking place in the castle's Great Hall.

Sir Neville sat with his chief guests at a high table on a platform at one end of the room, leering down at the knights seated at the tables below.

The hall was noisy, crowded and smelly. Every table buckled under the weight of food – soup and bread and fish and fowl and roasted swans and peacocks.

Servants scurried about to replenish sauces and jugs of wine.

Everybody ate with their fingers and used thick slices of stale bread called trenchers for plates. As they ate, acrobats entertained them, dogs crunched bones on the floor and Sir Neville's falcon watched everything with a bright and supercilious eye.

It watched Jo as Jeremiah Wormscrode dragged her up to the high table.

At the time, Sir Neville was helping himself to a peacock's wing and watching an acrobat perform a fire-eating triple somersault, so he gave them only a cursory grimace.

'What's up, Wormscrode?' he growled.

The steward cringed, and the trailing slug of his moustache slithered round his mouth. 'This, sire, is Joanne, a criminal,' he drooled. 'She's a runaway. Her parents are dead and she is your property, but she fled to deny you her service. I have brought her to you for punishment.'

'What do you suggest?' asked Sir Neville – rather vaguely, because he was more interested in waiting for the acrobat to burn his mouth off.

'I recommend the severest penalty, sire.'

The Wormscrode would have said more, but Jo shook him off and stormed up to the Maggot and said, 'Can I say something, your sirship, all ri'?'

Sir Neville was astonished. He looked at her now for the first time – irritably, as you might scowl at an annoying fly before swatting it to kingdom come.

'What?' he snapped.

Jo took a deep breath and repeated the words Walter had spoken only hours earlier. 'I claim trial by combat, an' I challenge this nasty man to a duel, 'cos he's my accuser. That's my right, en't it, your sirship?'

She poked her tongue out at Jeremiah, who spluttered and turned purple. His slug of a moustache squirmed. 'How dare you!' he slavered.

But Sir Neville cooed with delight. 'By gad, Wormscrode, here's another one with a nerve!' he snorted.

'You wouldn't agree, sire – would you?' Jeremiah squealed.

'Wouldn't I just! A chit of a girl against a fully grown weed – what a comical contest! We'll squeeze it in tomorrow between the jousting and the beheading. You've got a busy afternoon ahead of you. But what entertainment, eh, begad!'

Jo cleared her throat and crossed her fingers. 'There's just one more thing, all ri', your sirship,' she said. 'Since I'm only small I can choose a champion to fight for me, can't I?'

Sir Neville frowned. 'Well, that's in the rules, so I suppose you can. But who'd fight for *you*? You're nobody.'

'Mebbe I am,' Jo said humbly, 'an' mebbe I come from nowhere, but I got a champion anyhow. I'll bring him tomorrow. He's called Georgie.'

chapter Fifteen
Midsummer Madness

There is always something strange about Midsummer Eve. Magic floats on the air.

It was floating on the long midsummer evening of the Year of Our Lord 1305. The result was a kind of madness that affected everybody.

For some – like Peter Bullfinch, sprawled behind the wrestling ring soused in wine – it brought an enchantment which made even fairies seem possible.

For others – like Walter, Jo, Sir Harry le Frit and Robert of Swyre – it brought an anxiety about the morrow which caused the hours to hang like weights around their necks.

Everybody, happy or sad, felt the madness in some way.

But nobody felt it more than Big George.

He sat just inside the forest rim, looking out at a real live fairy tale.

As his eyes roved round the scene he saw that every pavilion and castle turret boasted a glittering pennant that fluttered and made the cheerful chuckling sound that falling water makes.

He saw the people's bright clothes catch the glow of the evening sun like coloured fires, and he saw the sunlight flash and dazzle on the armour of knights practising for the tourney.

At the same time, George heard interesting sounds everywhere: the clash of the knights' lances hitting the quintain, the happy shouts of children, dogs barking. He heard men and women calling and singing, and from inside the distant castle walls the ceaseless noise of blacksmiths forging and hammering new armour for the morrow.

On top of all this, he heard noises of merriment where jugglers, conjurors and tumblers were growing ever more daring as the heady wine took hold.

'Ooothmadderwoggglyy,' George whispered, awe-struck. It was magic.

Near at hand, though, something both solemn and comical was going on.

Walter and Sir Harry le Frit were practising

jousts. Jolting up and down on their nags, and hardly able to stay upright because of the weight of their armour, they tilted at one another – urging their horses into a gallop and desperately trying to unseat each other with their enormous lances.

They missed every time.

Jo ached with laughing, although she knew that really this was very serious because it could be a matter of life or death for both of them.

Especially for Walter.

'Walter expects to die tomorrer, you know, Georgie,' she said softly. 'He probably will too, because he'll fight clean even if everybody else fights dirty. Walter really believes in this chivalry stuff, see. He believes in courage an' truth an' gentleness an' honner and all the things knights are supposed to have. That's good, but it en't fair if the others don't play by the same rules. There en't nothin' gentle about gettin' your head knocked off, is there?'

Then she winked. 'Mind, yous can fight as dirty as yous like for me, so long as yous win, all ri'?'

They watched Walter and Sir Harry wearily lower their lances again, and charge again, and miss again, and fall from their horses with a juddering crash. They lay still on the ground, bruised and battered and exhausted.

'*We've* got to fight dirty for Walter tomorrer,' Jo whispered, 'yous an' me, and never mind what he wants. I dunno how, though. We'll have to make it up as we go along.'

She looked anxiously at George then, and prodded his arm. 'Georgie, are yous listenin' to me?'

George smiled. He didn't know what Jo meant, and he had no idea that he was supposed to fight for her tomorrow.

But he liked the sound of it.

It was all part of the magic and madness of this wonderful Midsummer Eve.

Chapter Sixteen
The Jousting Favour

Walter couldn't sleep. In the end he gave up trying and got up quietly. It was still very early. No one else was awake. A mist blanketed the pavilion field, hiding the lists and promising heat later on. It would be too hot inside his armour – although probably he wouldn't be inside it for long.

Walter sighed. He was extraordinarily nervous. His hands shook. He felt like crying, but that would be neither a manly nor a knightly thing to do, so he tried not to do it. Besides, it would shame his father.

The thought of his father almost broke him.

Today, they would see each other at last, briefly, before Death visited them both. Walter clenched his fists. He must put on a good show, to make his father proud and give him one thing at least to smile about.

But as he checked his equipment to make sure it was all in order, the handle of his lance below the fist guard dropped off.

Walter really could have cried then. He had just learned how to compensate for the lance's warp, but now it had given up the ghost altogether. That must have happened when he and Sir Harry fell off their horses last night.

It was clear that the Wormscrode had not only given him a worn-out horse and crumbling armour, but also a useless weapon.

Walter took a long, deep, shuddering breath. He would show him. Walter of Swyre would show everybody what a real squire could do. He wasn't sure how, but he'd do it.

He looked up then and saw Big George watching him.

George took the broken lance from his hand. He examined it carefully, then smiled.

'Goddit,' he said.

'What do you mean, 'goddit'?' Walter cried. 'It's too short now. My opponent's lance will have me off my horse before mine gets anywhere near him. I've no chance now.'

George took no notice. He chuntered to himself,

as if he was thinking out loud. Then he winked and put a finger against his nose and whispered conspiratorially, 'Dibdoo, Wallltterrrr.'

Walter gaped at him. 'Dibdoo?'

George nodded. 'Dibdoo.'

When Jo woke, her first thoughts were also about what the day might bring. Would she be back in the pillory by nightfall – or in the rat-infested dungeon beneath Castle Magott? Would Walter be alive? Would his father still have a head on his shoulders? And as for that amazing, wonderful grolyhoomp – what would happen to him?

It was all too frightening to think about, so Jo strolled across the dewy grass to Walter and George, looked out over the misty encampment and said, rather shyly, 'What are yous two goin' to do for favours?'

'Favours?' said Walter, surprised.

'Ffayyyvoos?' George repeated.

'Yous know very well, Walter,' said Jo, 'that knights allus fight for the honour of a lady. An' they carry her favour, as a token of her love. That's ri', en't it?'

'Well, yes, I suppose so,' said Walter uncertainly, 'but—'

Jo blushed. 'Then I reckon yous got to have favours like everybody else. It en't fair otherwise. Now I know I en't much like a real lady, an' prob'ly never will be, but I'm the only one yous got. So I'm gunna give each of yous a favour to carry, cos you're my knights, all ri'? The trouble is, I en't got much. So here goes . . .'

Before Walter could protest, Jo had torn the left sleeve off her dress and knotted it round his broken lance.

Walter felt embarrassed. 'I don't know what to say,' he mumbled.

'Then don't say anythin'. Go out there an' fight for your lady. Yous got to win now, 'cos that's a token. Now you're the Blue Knight.'

'The Blue Knight,' Walter repeated. 'I like that.'

'Ffayyyvoos,' said George.

'You're catching on quick,' Jo grinned. 'All right, Georgie, it's your turn now. This is for yous, 'cos you're my champion – you're gunna fight for me today, all ri'? I'll tell you when. Now bend down.'

She beckoned to him and George leaned down towards her. Then Jo took the ancient rabbit's foot from her neck, rubbed it between her thumb and forefinger for luck, and fastened it to George's tunic, over his heart.

'There, Georgie. Yous got a lady's favour too. It's like Tilly again, ri', only this time it's Jo – Nowhere Jo, eh.'

'Till-yyy.' George fingered the spoon in his pocket. Then he touched the rabbit's foot. 'Jooo.'

Jo grinned. 'Yous got ladies all over the place, yous naughty grolyhoomp. Now then, both of yous, stop wastin' time an' get out there an' fight. An' *win*, all ri'?'

chapter Seventeen
Knightly Ninepins

So began the strangest event in the entire history of knightly tournaments. Before long the sun rose and vanquished the mist. The people woke in their pavilions. Peter Bullfinch opened a bleary eye behind the wrestling ring, squinted at the light, groaned and scratched himself.

Midsummer Day had begun.

By nine o'clock the pavilion field was empty because everybody was crowding the boarded jousting lists to get a good view.

At nine-thirty the ladies, in richly embroidered dresses, climbed the steps to the stand, where they would have a perfect view of their heroes' triumphs and disasters.

At nine-forty-five Sir Neville de Magott arrived with his party and sat in the front row. A burly guard manacled a small, pale-faced man to the seat on his left. Immediately, a long-haired woman with a lovely but lined face pushed determinedly through the crowd and ran round the lists to join the prisoner. The guard tried to stop her but Sir Neville waved him away, and the woman sat beside the man and looked at him with love and fear.

Sir Neville leered at her and the ladies and waved rigid arms at his peasants. They cheered him, because like Citizen Martin of Swineytown they knew which side their bread was buttered, and Sir Neville said to himself, 'How pleasant it is to be popular! What a great man I am! And it all comes naturally! Well, let's not hang about, let the good times roll!'

He clapped his hands and fourteen trumpeters in golden livery marched forward and blew a noisy fanfare. The people cheered again, this time voluntarily because they were excited.

Then a Herald rode into the lists, reined in his horse in front of Sir Neville, unfurled a scroll and shouted, 'Oyez! Oyez! Whereas Sir Neville de Magott of Castle Magott has graciously commanded that a grand tourney shall be fought here this Midsummer Day in the Year of Our Lord 1305, we beg him graciously to give the signal to begin!'

The Herald rolled up his scroll and Sir Neville

leered graciously, rose stiffly to his feet, cranked up his right arm and dropped it. The people threw their caps in the air and yelled their heads off as to their left and right, at each end of the boarded enclosure, a heavily armoured horseman appeared.

The tournament was starting.

Already, though, there was something strange about it. Instead of growing silent in anticipation, the people began to snigger. Sir Neville frowned with annoyance, but when he gave the horsemen a second glance he tittered himself.

Soon everybody was in stitches – except the manacled man. His pale face flushed scarlet and he hung his head in shame, because he could see that one of those horsemen was his only son.

The other was Sir Harry le Frit.

It was sheer bad luck that Walter and Sir Harry had been drawn against each other in the first round – although it meant that one of them at least would progress to the second round, which was a marvel in itself.

To the onlookers the very appearance of these two contestants was a marvel – a gangling tin scarecrow pitted against a rusty midget with a torn blue sleeve dangling from his chopped off lance. You couldn't choose between them for clownishness.

'Joust!' cried the herald, to prevent the tournament descending into farce before it had even started. 'Charge!'

Walter gulped. He whispered a prayer, lowered his visor and spurred his horse forward.

Sir Harry le Frit gulped. For the first time in his jousting career he had hopes of winning a tilt. 'Watch this, Gwenny,' he squeaked, and spurred his horse into a gallop.

The horses' hooves thundered on the grass. The knights' armour rattled, and inside their helmets their heads rattled too.

Then, as they drew close to one another they raised their shields, lowered their lances and urged their horses even faster.

Walter gritted his teeth, closed his eyes and waited for the crash.

Sir Harry le Frit gritted his teeth, closed his eyes, and waited for the crash.

What happened next was a complete surprise, both to them and everybody else, because just when it seemed that Sir Harry's lance would pierce Walter like a stick in a toffee apple, he disappeared.

Faster than an eye can blink, the longest lance in the world – it might have been a pole, or perhaps a very thin tree – appeared out of nowhere and locked into the broken fist guard of Walter's lance. Faster still it thrust the lance forward, hooked it into Sir Harry le Frit's chainmail jacket and scooped him out of his saddle like the yolk out of an egg.

The crowd blinked, mystified.

Sir Neville de Magott was mystified.

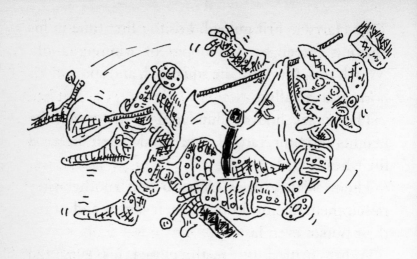

Jeremiah Wormscrode was mystified.

Robert of Swyre was mystified.

Walter, his son, was not just mystified. He was flabbergasted.

But Jo knew exactly what had happened. Lying low beside the grolyhoomp among the empty pavilions, she wriggled her toes with delight. 'Yous done it, Georgie,' she sang, 'yous saved Walter! But let Sir Harry down gently, all ri'?'

The grolyhoomp nodded and raised the thin tree like a fishing rod, swinging his wriggling catch high over the pavilions and dropping it at the forest rim. When Sir Harry le Frit opened his eyes at last he was very surprised to find himself in the arms of a bear.

The tournament went downhill from there – or uphill, depending on whose side you were on.

For Walter it passed in a blur.

He was aware that somehow Sir Harry le Frit had vanished, which meant that he must have won the first round. So he rode up to the stand and saluted Sir Neville and his father and mother, and he saw the love and pride in his parents' eyes and the anger in Jeremiah Wormscrode's.

After that, nothing made any sense at all.

Somehow, Walter's lance returned to his hand in time for him to face his second opponent, Ralph de Crackling. He saw Ralph bearing down on him, imagined the hatred in the piggy eyes behind the black visor, saw the black lance point at his heart. He spurred his own horse forward and lowered his lance.

Walter thought he must have shut his eyes again, because the next thing he knew there was an almighty clang and then a crash as Ralph hit the ground screaming.

Among the empty pavilions Nowhere Jo lowered her catapult. 'Two down, four to go, Georgie,' she grinned. 'It's fun, this, en't it?'

Knights went down like ninepins.

The third knight, a red-haired giant with a scarlet

shield, hardly knew what hit him, because at the moment he charged, Jo begged George to use the extraordinary talent she'd heard at the Ox's house party.

'Sing, Georgie!' she cried. 'Throw them bagpipes at 'im, loud as you like! Put 'im off 'is stride! Knock 'im down with music!'

To show what she meant she directed at the scarlet knight a piercing hoot, which sped through the air like an arrow of sound. George caught on immediately and fired a humming roar that made everybody in the lists throw themselves down and hold their ears to stop their heads bursting.

The Scarlet Knight couldn't do that. His helmet was in the way. Besides, his horse was already on the move – his joust had started.

But the sound was directed at *him*, and he took its full force. The thrumming noise flew into his helmet like a swarm of bees. The bees buzzed round and round his head, making him reel. They flew into his ears and fluttered crazily in there, whining and stinging.

The Scarlet Knight thought he was going mad. He cried out, dropped his lance and feverishly tried to undo his helmet. It wouldn't come off. It was stuck. He roared in frustration and beat the helmet with his mailed fists to dislodge the bees from his ears. He was doing that, knocking himself senseless, when Walter reached him.

All Walter had to do was tilt the knight out of his saddle, but as he drew close he crossed the sound path himself and the noise burst into his helmet, too, rattling his brain and making him so dizzy he almost missed.

Almost, but not quite. Wildly he swung his lance and clipped the knight's shoulder just as the Scarlet Knight dealt himself a knockout blow to the jaw.

The Scarlet Knight toppled from his horse and fell to the ground unconscious. George stopped singing, Jo clapped her hands in glee and the people looked up and saw Walter holding his lance high in triumph.

They were still wondering what had happened when Peter Bullfinch, as he had promised, entered the lists like a tornado. Using the famous whirling technique which so bewildered his wrestling opponents, he flailed his cannonball arms, lifted the Green Knight, Walter's next opponent, clean off his horse, and spun back out of the lists like a disappearing top. The knight hit the ground with a bone-shattering crash and stayed there. The next thing the crowd saw was Walter waving his lance in the air again.

Four down, two to go. Nobody had ever seen anything like it.

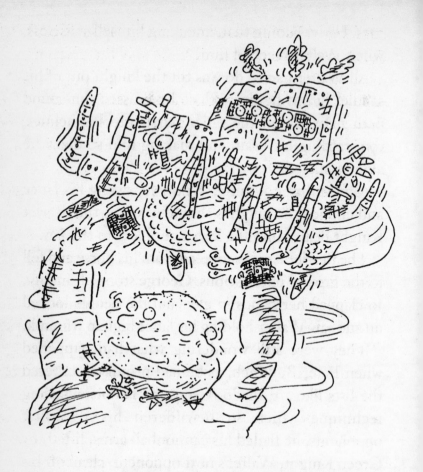

After each peculiar victory Walter rode up to the stand and saluted his smiling parents. The onlookers weren't laughing at him now. They were cheering.

Sir Neville leered viciously and ordered his steward to get on his horse and be prepared to bring this nonsense to an end.

But now Walter had to face his greatest

challenge. His next opponent was to be Sir Ribrub de Crackling, the Dark Knight and the reigning jousting champion.

Sir Ribrub wasn't going to take any nonsense from a renegade boy. He stormed into the lists in a fury, slammed down his visor and set off immediately towards the little upstart.

But the little upstart wasn't ready.

The midsummer sun was beating down, and inside Walter's armour the temperature felt like a thousand degrees. His skin prickled. Sweat streamed through his hair and into his eyes as he cantered wearily back into the lists and lowered his lance.

Only then did he realise his foe was already charging at him full tilt. And only then did he realise who it was.

The shock all but unseated Walter. He slipped sideways in his saddle. Dizzily, he tried to pull himself upright again, but it was all he could do to hang on and not fall. Upside-down, he watched Sir Ribrub's lance hurtle towards him, fast as a javelin, with death on its tip.

For Jo and Big George, what happened next was pure inspiration.

'Do somethin', Georgie!' Jo shrieked.

'Ssommthhnnn,' George hummed.

'Now, ri'?'

'Nowwry.'

'*Georgie!*'

Galvanised into action, George grabbed Jo in his fist, thrust her over the heads of the crowd and put her down on the neck of the Dark Knight's horse, facing him.

'How are yous, mister?' said Jo, smiling sweetly as she tore off her right sleeve and stuffed it into Sir Ribrub's visor. 'Nice day, en't it?'

Sir Ribrub de Crackling was not just blinded, he was so surprised he forgot what he was doing. By the time he remembered, he was two miles away and too late. And by then, of course, Jo was long gone – in fact she'd come and gone so quickly she was just a blue blur and nobody else appeared to have noticed her.

Sir Ribrub thought she must have been a fairy.

Five down, one to go.

Walter was still hanging upside-down in his saddle as he saluted the beaming Robert and scowling Maggot and prepared to meet his last opponent – Jeremiah Wormscrode, the cause of all his family's misery. He was so tired he hardly knew where he was any more.

But the Wormscrode knew very well.

He cantered up to the stand on a glistening chocolate-coloured horse and bowed to Sir Neville with a toadying stoop. His fat lips blossomed into a smile. 'Sire,' he drooled, 'your next champion pays you honour.'

Turning to the prisoner, he bowed mockingly and waved the point of his lance within an inch of Robert of Swyre's face.

'The next time you see this,' he snarled, 'it will have your son's head on it.'

Then Jeremiah Wormscrode took up his position in the lists and closed his visor with a snap.

'Time to do one more deed, Georgie,' Jo whispered urgently. 'Only I've run out of ideas, so it's up to you, all ri'? Walter is up against his worst enemy now. Can you think of anythin' to save 'im?'

George scratched his head. He looked puzzled. Then his eyes gleamed and his beard parted in a slow, enormous grin.

'Ssavve Walterrr,' he said, nodding and smacking his lips.

Smacking his lips is how Big George did it.

You know how, if you suck in your breath really sharply, you can drawn up something light from a table, like a feather or a fly?

That is what George did now.

It was a great trick, so great that nobody knew what happened – except Jeremiah, and even he was confused.

One second he was crowing and cantering and sighting along his lance at an upstart boy, with every intention of skewering him to kingdom come, and the next he felt himself hurtling through the air and landing in a wiry bush in attractive shades of blue and green.

He was trying to slide out of it when he looked down and noticed that he was a long, long way from the ground. So, gurgling with fright and slavering spit by the bucketful, he grabbed the wires and hung on.

As he dangled he looked up into two deep, dark, hairy tunnels.

These seemed to be sucking at him too, because every odd second he was drawn up towards them and every even second he was pushed down again. He felt like a puppet bobbing on a string.

It was a nightmare. He didn't know which was the more terrifying, the tunnels or the drop. But he did know that he couldn't hang on for much longer, because the weight of his armour was pulling him down.

Jeremiah Wormscrode felt the wire slipping

through his fingers. He whimpered. Then, just when he was sure things couldn't get any worse, they did.

An abyss opened up in front of his face.

It was dark, hot and humid, like staring into the mouth of a volcano. Then, like a volcano erupting, the abyss belched out an extraordinary roar which sounded – unless he was very much mistaken – like 'grolyhoomp'.

But Jeremiah Wormscrode had no time to consider this because now he was flying again, in reverse this time, blown instead of sucked.

He soared above the pavilions, planed down over the peasants' heads, missed his horse by a mile and landed slap in the lap of Sir Neville de Magott.

chapter Eighteen
The Seventh Knight

Sir Neville wasn't himself after that.

But Jeremiah was worse – he was gibbering. Tears of terror drenched his cheeks. He threw himself on the ground, clutched Sir Neville's knees and wailed, 'Forgive me, sire, for I have sinned! I've been to the jaws of hell and back but I know that can only be the beginning of my punishment! Oh, sire, I confess! I confess!'

'Confess to what?' gasped Sir Neville, trying to pull his body back into shape.

'Why, sire, to everything!'

'*Everything?*'

'Everything! Because everything I have ever done has been wicked! Let me confess, sire, please!'

'Oh, very well, if you must,' said Sir Neville – rather absently, because he was seeing if he knew what day of the week it was, to judge whether he needed to pull his head into shape as well. 'Confess away.'

That is precisely what Jeremiah Wormscrode did. He owned up to every lie, theft, fraud, betrayal, assault, kidnap and murder he had committed since the day he was born. It took hours and became very boring.

Sir Neville was amazed that one man could get through so many misdeeds in a single lifetime. 'Let me get this straight, Wormscrode,' he yawned, as soon as he could get a word in. 'Are you saying you're a crook?'

'That sums it up nicely, sire.'

'And Robert of Swyre is innocent?'

'Absolutely.'

'Well, I'll be blowed,' Sir Neville said.

While the Wormscrode was confessing his sins, Walter too was trying to pull himself together.

He had finally fallen right out of his saddle and was lying sprawled on the grass, too bruised and tired to get up.

Then Peter Bullfinch, singing 'C'mon now, c'mon now, what's the madder wid you?' hauled him to his feet and propelled him towards the stand. 'Don't mess wid me, Walter,' the Ox whispered. 'You go up to that Maggot and claim your prize.'

Staggering the last few steps on his own Walter ignored the weeping Jeremiah, clanked up to Sir Neville, swayed, removed his helmet, bowed and croaked, 'Sir, as victor in this tournament and trial by combat, I claim my father's freedom.'

'Do you, by jove?' said Sir Neville.

'Freedom, yiss!' a girl's voice shouted from somewhere among the empty pavilions. 'Give 'im freedom, all ri'?'

And an extraordinary humming voice, which vibrated the air like the drone from a thousand bagpipers, echoed 'Ffreeem! Ffreeeeeemm!'

Now the people took up the cry. 'Robert of Swyre is innocent!' they shouted. 'Make him Steward again and execute the Wormscrode instead!'

'I say,' cried Sir Neville, 'that's a good idea!'

Jeremiah Wormscrode took the hint at record speed. He leaped the lists and was streaking through the pavilions before anyone could stop him.

Only Jo, standing on George's head, saw what happened next. Only she knew that, quick though the steward was, the grolyhoomp's boot was even quicker, and that was why Jeremiah Wormscrode turned into a human rocket that whooshed out of the pavilions and crashed deep inside the forest.

When he arrived there the bear, who was very hungry, grunted for joy and began chasing him.

She may be chasing him still.

Then Jo watched the burly guard loosen the manacles from Robert of Swyre. A lump lodged in her throat when she saw that pale, gentle man step forward to embrace his son, and she knew from the way they clasped each other that both were weeping.

Now the crowd took up a new cry.

'Honour the boy!' they shouted. 'Honour the new champion!'

Jo leaped recklessly from George's head and raced towards the lists. 'Yiss, yous do that, yous old Maggot!' she shouted. 'Yous give Walter honner, all ri'?'

Sir Neville looked uncertainly at his people. They were overexcited, jumping up and down like yapping dogs in a hunt. When dogs get like that, he thought, you can't trust them – they'll turn on you and bite if you aren't careful. And these dogs seem determined to have their way, and here's that ragged girl inciting them still further. Better give in for now. Just for now.

So, Sir Neville, being a coward at heart, beckoned Walter to come to him.

Jo reached the stand just in time to see Walter

kneel and Sir Neville, leering like a lunatic, dub
him on the shoulder with his sword and say, 'Arise,
Sir Knight.'

The crowd cheered, the ladies simpered and Jo –

who really was no lady – threw herself at Walter, flung her arms round his neck and kissed him.

Walter was so surprised he fell over again.

When he'd recovered he squinted up at her grinning face and said, 'Will you tell me something, Jo?'

'Anythin'.'

'What's going on?'

'Everythin's goin' on,' she smiled. 'An' it's all good an' it's all because of that grolyhoomp!'

But everything was not good, because like a wicked magician Sir Neville had one last nasty trick up his sleeve.

He whispered to the herald, and the herald marched forward and cried, 'Oyez! Oyez! SILENCE! Sir Neville de Magott wishes to make an announcement!'

When the people had quietened, Sir Neville grimaced and shouted, 'We may be denied an execution but our entertainment isn't over yet. Neither is the tournament. Because, my people, I decree a seventh round! This renegade . . .' Here he clamped an icy hand round Jo's shoulder, 'has chosen trial by combat to prove her innocence. Her champion's adversary was to be that grovelling ninny Wormscrode, but since he's run away we shall have to choose another foe to replace him. What say you?'

'We say *aye*!' the people shouted, as eager as ever to see blood spilt.

'And who better,' leered the Maggot, 'than our new champion?'

'Aye! Aye! Aye!' Caps soared skywards. Feet stamped the ground. 'Let Walter of Swyre be the Seventh Knight! Let him prove he's a true knight – make him fight once more!'

Jo gaped at Walter in dismay.

Walter stared at her in horror.

'Who's your champion, Jo?' he asked in a shaky voice. 'It couldn't be . . . could it?'

Jo nodded. 'Who else?'

Walter's eyes rolled.

'Call your champion, girl,' Sir Neville commanded.

Jo brushed away tears. 'What shall I do?'

'You have no choice,' said Walter, struggling to his feet. 'You must call him.'

'But how you gunna fight a grolyhoomp?'

'I've no idea. Anyway, I don't want to fight George. He's my friend. Perhaps he'll think of something.'

Jo gazed across the pavilion field. There was no sign of Big George – he was keeping well hidden, as they'd agreed. Well, that was futile now.

She took a deep breath. 'Georgie,' she cried, 'show yourself!'

George did.

But it wasn't at all in the way they expected.

Chapter Nineteen
Champion George

Something was happening to George. He was gripped by a very odd idea. It was while he watched the loving reunion between Walter and his father that it suddenly occurred to him that he might be dreaming.

Because wasn't it only yesterday – or even today – that he had woken up in a strange forest and discovered an extremely small girl called Tilly, and after a most peculiar adventure lost her again?

And wasn't it soon afterwards that his rest had been disturbed by another very small person, the boy whose extraordinary quest was ending here?

It was bewildering, because in the huge timespan of George's life, earthly days seemed to pass in a blink, and yet so many things happened in them it made him dizzy to think about it.

How was anybody to make sense of a conundrum like that, other than to think it was all a dream?

But if he was dreaming he must be sleepwalking.

And if he was sleepwalking, where was his bedroom, and his bed?

That is how it came about that at exactly the moment Jo shouted to him, George stood up to look for his bedroom – and saw in the distance a rounded hill that seemed familiar.

He decided to have a closer look at it.

Whether George understood what was happening in the lists is anybody's guess. Yet what happened now was extraordinarily apt. You might say it worked like a dream. The sight of a forty-foot-high grolyhoomp rising out of their tents like a genie out of a lamp gave the tournament spectators quite a start. They cried out in terror. Many fell to their knees. Others fainted clean away. They all liked excitement, but they'd had that already and this was one thrill too many.

'Help!' yelped Sir Neville, 'is *that* your champion, girl?'

'That's him all ri',' Jo nodded. 'Big, en't he?'

'He certainly is. But what's he doing? Why is he walking away?'

Jo, who had no idea what George was doing, said confidently, 'He's getting hisself ready, I expect.'

But she frowned and glanced at Walter, who shrugged helplessly.

'Georgie!' Jo cried. 'Come back!'

Walter shook his lance and shouted, 'Come on now, grolyhoomp, come and fight! Don't mess with me, now!'

When George finally stopped he was so far out of the lists he seemed to have shrunk almost to human size. There he waited while Walter, helped by Peter Bullfinch and Sir Harry le Frit, who had just arrived back from the forest, hauled himself up on to the despairing heap of bones that was his horse, dropped his visor like the clang of fate, and rode out for one last joust.

At last, he was ready. The Seventh Knight faced Jo's distant champion. And Big George faced him.

Sir Neville raised his arm.

The chief trumpeter raised his trumpet.

The people held their breath.

The herald drew his breath in.

Any second now.

Jo closed her eyes, pictured the rabbit's foot on George's chest and frantically rubbed it in her mind for luck. When she opened them again she had the strangest impression that events were happening in slow motion, like a dream . . .

She saw Sir Neville's arm fall like a lazy feather.

She heard a long, lingering trumpet note, and the drawn-out cry of 'Oye-e-e-ez!' from the herald.

She saw Walter spur his nag forward and she saw George start to run.

But even in slow motion George was running amazingly fast. He zoomed out of the distance at a hundred miles an hour, growing larger and faster with every pounding step.

The people cowered.

The leer froze on Sir Neville de Magott's face.

Walter's horse whinnied with terror and reared up on its hind legs, pawing the air with its hooves as if warding off an evil spirit.

And Big George, thundering forward, gave out the most amazing war cry anyone anywhere has ever heard.

'Zzzunkerrsmitkinnfuongerrumpterrighttsniggleoo opstengrollsmoglewwwtroggly!' he roared at the top of his voice – which, more or less, is grolyhoomp-speak for 'I spy with my little eye, something beginning with B!'

Nobody knew that, of course.

All Walter knew was that his horse was

performing a two-hooved dance and the ground was shaking and George was bearing down on him like doom on legs. There were only a hundred yards between them now.

Seventy-five.

Fifty.

The way his horse was prancing it was impossible for Walter to use his lance. So he screamed instead.

'Aaaaahh!' he shouted.

'Aaaaaaaaaaaaaaaaaaaahhhhaaaaa!' replied George, tipping the Seventh Knight an enormous wink as he thundered past at about a thousand miles a minute.

After that, George paid no more attention to Walter or Jo or the other midgets than if they had been the figments of a dream.

With his great loping strides he was far away from them in no time at all, a diminishing figure racing towards the afternoon sun and a curious hump-backed hill.

Then, suddenly, he vanished.

chapter Twenty
arise, Sir Grolyhoomp

Believing that Walter had chased away a giant which had threatened all their lives, the people paraded him on their shoulders like a hero, up and down the lists for the next hour.

But Walter's victory was Jo's defeat. She had lost her trial by combat.

Sir Neville called her over to him for sentencing.

'From now on,' he growled, contriving a leer so grotesque Jo thought his face was dividing in two, 'you will be the property of my steward Robert of Swyre, to dwell in his house and do his bidding until your life's end. Do you understand?'

Jo nodded dumbly. Choking back a sob, she looked wildly for an escape route but found none.

She was back where she had started.

'Come to your new master, girl.'

Robert of Swyre was beckoning to her. His wife Mary held his hand and their son Walter stood beside them like a battered tin soldier, grinning broadly – smirking at Jo's misery, no doubt.

Jo wasn't having that, so with dark eyes blazing she marched up to Walter and cried, 'I en't gunna do no bidding from yous, all ri'? I en't your serf. Yous don't own me!'

Walter smiled infuriatingly. 'I never said I did.'

'Nobody owns you, Joanne,' said Walter's father, in a voice that was at once warm, soft, calm and astonishing.

'*What?*' she gasped.

Robert of Swyre smiled. 'You saved my son's life. That means you helped save mine too. In return, I can do no less than give you what you most desire. From this moment you are a free person.'

Jo couldn't speak. She stared at him like an idiot.

'Go on, father,' said Walter.

Robert of Swyre let go of his wife's hand and gently but firmly took Jo's in his strong fist. 'I believe you like to be called Joanne of Nowhere. Is that so?'

'Well, I . . . yiss . . . I suppose I do,' Jo babbled. 'But that's because—'

'From now on, would you do us the honour of becoming Joanne of Swyre, and living with us in our home?'

Jo felt dizzy. This couldn't be happening. 'Living with yous as what?' she whispered.

'As family, Jo. As our daughter and Walter's sister. Well, what do you say?'

Jo's eyes filled with tears. The lump was in her throat again. She felt stupid. But truly there were no words, no words. She looked helplessly at Walter.

Walter beamed.

'She says all ri',' he said.

Next morning, very early, Walter and Jo tiptoed

from the sleeping house and started to run. They were on a mission, Walter said.

'What sort of mission? Where's we going?' Jo asked him, but Walter said it was a secret, which was infuriating but exciting too.

He led her through the fields with their chequered crops, past the jutting forest rim and across a great wasteland towards that distant, curiously rounded hill. When they drew near Jo saw that it was clad in bushes and low trees, and covered by an enormous briar rose.

At its foot Walter put a finger to his lips and whispered, 'We have to climb. No talking now.'

It was very steep. As they pulled themselves up Jo saw that Walter was searching for something.

Higher they went, and higher. For a moment, Walter seemed anxious, but then he grunted, 'Over there', and headed towards a bush whose roots were raised slightly from the ground. He peeled away the turf beneath it and uncovered a hole.

Jo shivered. 'We en't going down there, are we?'

Walter nodded, lowered himself into the hole and disappeared.

Muttering a prayer, Jo followed – and dropped like a stone on to something that was neither hard nor soft but rose and fell like waves on a beach.

She had expected it to be dark, but an eerie green

glow to her right made her heart miss a beat. She'd seen that light before, coming from Big George's face!

'What's he doing?' she breathed.

Walter, sitting beside her on what she now realised was George's chest, whispered, 'He's sleeping. This is how I found him. I woke him up and asked him to help me. Well he's done that, so now he's come back to rest again. I thought that was probably what had happened, but I had to make sure he was all right.'

'What happens now?'

'Nothing. We have to let him sleep.'

Jo gave a little shriek. 'I don't want to leave him here!'

Walter frowned. 'He doesn't belong out there, Jo. I mean, have you ever seen a grolyhoomp out in the open before?'

Jo shook her head sadly. 'He belonged to us, though, didn't he?'

'Maybe, for a short time. But I wouldn't like to trust him to anyone else. He's too important.'

In her heart Jo knew Walter was right, but she didn't give up easily. 'Before we go I want to whisper somethin' to him, all ri'? It's a secret.'

'Very well. But be quick. I don't want anyone seeing us leave.'

Walter moved away and Jo, wiping her eyes, climbed up to George's face and leaned towards his ear.

'Georgie,' she breathed, 'can yous hear me?'

There was no response. He was asleep all right.

So Jo did what she was determined to do. Holding her arm stiff she reached out her hand and touched Big George's shoulder as if her finger was the tip of a sword.

'I knight yous, Georgie,' she whispered, ''cos yous deserves it, all ri'? So, arise, Sir Grolyhoomp!'

George slumbered on.

Jo looked at him for a long while, then returned to Walter. 'What do we do next?' she asked him.

'Close up the hill so nobody can find him.'

'Let's do it then. What yous waitin' for?'

As they climbed back into the world they heard George give an enormous snore. It made them laugh, and laughing made them feel better about leaving him.

As they replaced the roots and then the turf so carefully that afterwards even they couldn't find the entrance again, Jo said hopefully, 'He might come out again tomorrer, mightn't he? After he's slept a bit?'

Walter smiled at her persistence. 'Yes, Jo,' he said gently. 'Perhaps he will. Come on, let's go home.'

After that Jo, Walter, Robert and Mary, all of Swyre, lived very happily together.

Robert became once more the honest steward to Sir Neville de Magott that he had been before. He grew to be his trusted friend, too, and was able to influence him in many good ways – even to relax a little and stop leering quite so crazily.

Walter returned to his studies. In time, he

became one of the greatest knights in the land, and a renowned jousting champion – although never again did he achieve quite such a triumph as the time when a grolyhoomp called George gave him a hand.

And Jo? Well, Jo soon changed her mind about wanting to be a lady. After all the excitement she'd had with Big George, that seemed too tame for words. Instead, she decided that *she* could become a knight too, because, as she told Walter, 'Anythin' yous can do, I can do too, all ri'?'

And Walter had to agree.

So Jo became the first girl ever to go to Knight School.

But that's another story.

afterword

Three things remain to be said.

The first may concern you, and it is this.

Although this story may seem to have happened a very long time ago, it's not so long ago really. Think of it this way. Like Tilly Miller before them, when Jo and Walter grew up they both married and had children of their own. And their children had children, and their children's children had children, on through the generations right up to today – and perhaps to you.

So you see, there's a big possibility that you yourself may be connected to the tale of Big George *and the* Seventh Knight.

The second thing concerns Big George.

He returned to his hill to carry on with his rudely interrupted sleep, but that hill is quite a puzzle. It began life as a dome made to look natural, and as the centuries passed it grew more and more to look like a real hill. But it never was a real hill. It still isn't.

So keep your eyes peeled. If you see a hill that looks like a hill but isn't a hill, you may be getting warm. If it has a wild briar rose growing on it, listen for snores.

The third thing concerns both you and George, and it's this.

Remember that the inhabitants of a star hidden deep inside the constellation of Ursa Middling sleep for exactly nine hundred Earth years. Add 900 to 1103 – the year Big George first fell asleep – and what do you get?

You get shivers running up your spine and your hair standing on end, because you could have a grolyhoomp knocking at your door the day after tomorrow, wanting breakfast.

Be sure to have some ready for him.